LISA

ARLENE HALE

SCHOLASTIC BOOK SERVICES
New York Toronto London Auckland Sydney Tokyo

Cover Photo by Owen Brown

ISBN 0-590-32001-7

12 11 10 9 8 7 6 5 4 3 2   2 3 4 5 6/8

LISA

A Wildfire Book

WILDFIRE TITLES
FROM SCHOLASTIC

Chapter 1 _____

The Centerville bleachers were packed with cheering fans. Insects crashed noisily against the green glow of the field lights. Lisa Holden was conscious of gripping her fists tightly as she watched Brad come to the plate. It was all up to him now.

"Come on, Brad!" she whispered. "Come on!"

The pitcher was taking his time, trying to make Brad nervous. Brad stepped out, knocked the dirt out of his cleats, looked up at the scoreboard, and then stepped in again. At last the pitch!

Smack! The bat hit the ball solidly, and everyone was on their feet. A mighty cheer went up as the ball kept sailing, sailing, sailing! A home run! Brad rounded the bases with his graceful, long-legged lope. As he came toward home, the cheers were deafening. With his quick grin he lifted his cap to the crowd, the wind stirring his thick, blond hair. Lisa thought she couldn't bear the excitement. The game was over! With one swing of his bat Brad had lived up to his image of all-star athlete. Only a boy like Brad could have saved the game for Centerville, and in the process won them the state championship!

Beside Lisa, Tammy and Randy were shouting hoarsely and pounding each other on the back. All the Centerville fans were clapping and waving their banners in the air. Lisa felt the tears trickle down her cheeks. Brad! Oh, wonderful Brad! Her heart swelled until she thought it would burst with pride.

After the presentation of trophies, everyone thronged toward the team to offer their congratulations. It seemed everyone swarmed over Brad. He accepted their congratulations with a cool aplomb. Brad had been confident all along that they would win. Winning was not new to him.

Finally Lisa was able to reach him. "Brad!"

He laughed down into her blue eyes. "Told you we'd do it," he said.

"*You* did it," she said fervently. "Brad, I'm so proud of you."

Randy and Tammy pushed closer, too, and Randy thumped Brad on the back. "Good going, man!"

"It was wonderful," Tammy sighed. "I nearly died out there, watching."

"Listen, we all knew Brad would do it. Doesn't he always?" Randy asked. "Don't forget we've got the party at the Pizza Parlor. Boy, will we have reason to celebrate now!"

"Everybody's roarin' to go," Brad laughed. "Listen, give me a second — I'll get out of this uniform, shower, and hang up the cleats. Be with you as soon as I can."

But it was a struggle for Brad to make his way toward the high school gymnasium and the locker room, for everyone wanted to touch him or shake his hand. Brad was always the hero, the golden boy of Centerville High. Lisa laughed happily, enjoying the moment, finding herself, as Brad's girl, swept up into the glory as well.

"Fantastic!" someone called to her.

"Only way to go!" another shouted.

Lisa glowed. She shook her sunlit blonde hair and lifted her chin, relishing the thought that once again Brad had shown how really wonderful he was.

Lisa waited in Brad's car with Randy and Tammy, and when Brad finally came, hair damp from the shower, he leaped in beside them with a yell of delight.

"Hey, we're off! Boy, what a night this has been!"

Randy joined in the cheer. "What a way to end the school year! Man, did you see how flattened those cocky guys from West Dale were? They're always such hot shots! Didn't reckon on the likes of you, Brad."

Brad gave another shrug as he put the car in reverse and shot them out of the parking lot and, with a spin of the wheels, into the line of traffic.

"Just got lucky, that's all."

"My, my, modesty becomes you!" Randy teased, punching him in the ribs. "Come on, man, let's get this show on the road!"

It seemed half of the spectators had come to join them at the Pizza Parlor, their usual hangout. It was already crowded with all the team members and their friends.

Everyone tried to lure Brad away.

"Hey, come join us at our table, Brad!" they called.

Brad gave them a wave of his hand, but declined. Keeping his arm around Lisa, they stood for a moment as another cheer went up, Brad's name dancing on the air.

Lisa flushed with pleasure, enjoying all the flurries of attention.

"Hey, Lisa!"

Jody Johnson had managed somehow to wiggle in close to them. Jody gave Lisa a shy grin. Jody lived next door, and once when they were in pigtails and their big interest was roller skates, they had been friends. Since then they had gone separate ways. Jody was shy and quiet and seldom went out, but Lisa had suddenly become very popular once Brad began to date her. Now they were "the" couple in school, and Jody was well aware of the fact. It embarrassed Lisa that Jody was trying to tag after her, now of all times!

"Listen, wouldn't you and Brad come and join Gail and me? I mean, I've been telling Gail we were old friends."

Jody broke off with a foolish little laugh, flushing.

"Brad's expected to sit with the team," Lisa said. "Sorry."

She turned away and gripped Brad's arm tighter, wishing Jody would take the hint and go back to her mousy friend, Gail.

"Is she trying to make waves again?" Brad wondered in a whisper.

"Jody means well, I suppose."

"She's creepy," Brad said with a little frown between his magnificent blue eyes. "You know how she bugs me."

They were welcomed at the main table with another cheer. Brad waved and shouted back to them, holding up his fingers in a V shape, waving the

4

victory sign at everyone. To their chagrin they saw there was no room for Randy and Tammy. Looking angry, Brad motioned with his arm.

"Hey, you guys down there, shove over, will you? I want my buddies here with me."

Everyone scrambled to accommodate, and all of them were seated close together, laughing.

Lisa heard one disparaging note. "The golden one has spoken so everyone has to bust a gut!"

Lisa's face burned red, and she turned about quickly to see who had dared say such an ugly and disloyal thing. But there was no time to worry about one sour note. It was a night of nights! One to remember! She felt the glow come burning across her heart again, brushing a light into her blue eyes, tingeing every peal of her laughter.

"Listen, Brad, we're going to throw a bash at my house," Tinker Brown said, coming up to talk into Brad's unwilling ear. "Just a few friends. Why don't you come by?"

"Don't count on it," Brad said with a shrug. "Can't make it."

Tinker tried to hide his disappointment, but finally walked away as Brad turned his attention to someone else.

That was only one of the invitations they received to private celebrations. Brad refused them all, giving the three of them a wink. "We've got our own plan, right?"

"Better believe it," Randy chimed in. "Listen, don't you think we could blow now? Haven't you had enough of this?"

"Sure," Brad nodded. "But I have to hang around a little while . . . otherwise . . ."

Lisa gave him an adoring smile. It was like Brad to be aware of his own importance, to be concerned with the team, in not letting them down. He was the star, and everyone wanted him there. But she knew underneath that, just as much as she, he was dying to leave.

Finally they left the Pizza Parlor, and every eye seemed to follow them as they walked out. Brad kept his arm around Lisa's shoulder, and she loved the solid feel of his strength, the long strides he took. He was several inches taller than she; she had to look up at him, and she knew how handsome he was. She absolutely adored the slope of his jaw and his firm lips, his deep-set blue eyes peering out from under his thick blond eyebrows. His hair was almost wheat-colored, but with the summer sun it would bleach out to a pale yellow. Like a golden god. *Her* golden god! Heavens, how much she loved him!

They roared away from the Pizza Parlor, the twin pipes of Brad's car rippling with noisy, dangerous vibes. With a laugh they left the hangout, and without a word to anyone Brad nosed the car out of Centerville.

"Where are we going?" Tammy asked.

"Where else?" Brad wondered, reaching an arm to pull Lisa closer to him. "There's a cooler in the trunk, and the stars are out. Ought to be a perfect night at the lake."

Randy nodded agreement. "Man, oh, man, this will be a night to remember."

"Hate to be a wet blanket," Tammy sighed. "But you know I have to be in by midnight."

"Tonight?" Randy howled with disgust.

6

"*Every* night. You know the rules, and after the last time I'm not anxious to get my father mad at me again!"

Lisa stiffened in Brad's arms. The truth was, she was glad Tammy had mentioned the deadline. Hers was the same. Brad knew it, had always known it, but he sometimes got her home late.

"They know you're with me. No sweat," he always argued.

Unfortunately her parents didn't see it that way. For reasons she could never understand, they weren't completely sold on Brad, even though he was the most outstanding boy in school. It didn't make sense to her and never would.

"Okay, okay, Tammy," Brad grumbled. "We'll get you home before you turn into a pumpkin!"

"Silly, it was the coach that turned into a pumpkin," Lisa laughed.

They sped through the night and soon reached the banks of the lake.

"We've arrived," Brad said. "Everybody out. Look at that water. Hey, anybody for a swim?"

"It's not that warm," Randy said with a shiver and a shake of his head.

"No swim suits," Lisa said. "Besides, after that game you played, you must be about ready to drop."

Brad grinned and with a laugh swept her up in his arms to swing her around and around. "Think so, do you? Well, we'll see about that."

He carried her to the very edge of the water, and she began to yell as he threatened to toss her in.

"One for the money, two for the show —" he chanted, swinging her farther and farther over the water.

7

She pounded him with her fists, pleading with him, tugging at his hair. Finally with a laugh he stopped and pulled her into his arms.

"If I remember right, you promised me a kiss if we won tonight. I'll collect now, please."

She lifted her face for his long, sweet kiss.

"Hey, break it up," Randy yelled. "Let's open the cooler and have a cold drink. I'm dying of thirst."

Reluctantly Brad let her go, and they walked back to join Randy and Tammy. They opened cold bottles of soda, and from somewhere a large bag of chips appeared.

"Let's sit on the dock," Brad suggested.

"Oh, yes, I love it there," Lisa said.

It was a magical time. They sat on the wooden dock, swinging their feet out over the water as it sighed against the shore, caressing it, floating away, drifting back. Rhythmically. Slush, slush, slush. The moon, a silver round balloon with smudges across its face where lunar mountains rose, snuggled against the black sky.

Brad put his arm around Lisa's shoulder, and she dropped her head against him. His lips brushed her hair.

Brad lifted Lisa's face. He kissed her lips fleetingly, and in the dark she thought she could see the triumphant glow in his eyes.

"I'll never forget tonight," he said.

"Hail the conquering hero!" Tammy burst out with a giggle. "Brad did it again. He saved the game, the team, the school."

8

"Oh, stop it!" Lisa joined in. "He'll get a swelled head."

"Knock it off — all of you," Brad said, but he didn't mean it. He loved the praise because he knew he deserved it. He and Lisa had talked about it once.

"Okay, so I'm good at what I do, whether it's football, baseball, track — so okay, I'm good," he'd said. "I'm glad of it. I'd hate to be a deadbeat like some of the other guys. Is it wrong to be proud of yourself?"

And the way he'd said it, Lisa knew it wasn't. He was right. He *was* special. Knowing it didn't make him any less so! It annoyed her when, at that precise moment, her thoughts shifted to Jody. Edging toward them shyly tonight, watching them hopefully, her enthusiasm and anxiety written all over her face. Jody couldn't take a hint! Their special friendship had died ages ago. Jody didn't belong with Lisa's crowd, she could never fit in with Tammy and Randy. Brad disliked her for the very fact that she was so serious about everything.

It was just last week that Jody had come over to see her. Mother had sent her up to her room. Once, as mere kids, they had giggled together and told their secrets to each other in that room. Now Jody seldom came, for they had practically nothing in common. Lisa couldn't remember the last time she'd been in Jody's house, and she'd been startled when Jody suddenly appeared in the doorway.

"Hi," Jody said with her slow grin. "Your mother said it was okay to come up."

Mother would, she thought angrily. Mother thought Jody was a nice girl, that she had good sense and a certain shyness that was attractive. Little did Mother know! Jody was a big zero with Lisa's crowd.

"What are you doing?" Jody asked curiously.

"Trying to find a new way to do my hair."

"For the disco Friday night?"

"Yes, are you going?"

Jody flushed. "No. You know I've got two left feet. Besides, I'll be working at the hospital until eight."

Lisa's mouth made a straight line. She was sick to death of hearing about Jody's volunteer work. Jody sang its praises every chance she got, and worse yet, Dad thought Jody's contribution nothing short of super.

"Look, Jody, you're not going to lay that on me again, are you?" Lisa frowned.

"You'd be great, Lisa. With your bubbly personality the patients would love you!"

Lisa scoffed. "Not a chance."

"But with your father a doctor I'd think you'd *really* be interested —"

"That's just it!" Lisa said crossly. "Who wants to be under their father's nose all the time? Besides, I've heard hospital talk all my life."

"But Lisa, you'd love it! It makes you feel so . . . so . . ."

Jody broke off, stumbling for the right words. Poor Jody, she never could put what she felt into words. Maybe that was why she was always so shy and withdrawn. It was nearly impossible to picture her at the hospital, talking to total strangers!

10

"It makes you feel what?" Lisa demanded.

Jody gave a shrug, her eyes filled with compassion. "It makes you feel good about yourself."

"Oh, that!" Lisa sniffed. "Who needs it? I feel great about myself now. My life's great."

Jody's cheeks burned red. "That's right, I suppose it is. I guess you feel you don't need anything else, being Brad's girl and everything. Okay. Skip it. Sorry."

And Jody had fled like a frightened bird. The interruption had upset Lisa for no real reason at all. But why was she thinking of such a silly thing now of all times, with the perfect night on the lake and Brad so close to her?

"When do you start working at the swimming pool?" she asked him.

Brad straightened. Landing the lucrative summer job at the city swimming pool as lifeguard had pleased him. Everyone was impressed. She could picture him sitting high in his observation chair, watching the swimmers with his cool efficiency, his body sun-bronzed, his shoulders solid and square, his legs slim and strong. She could see him blowing his silver whistle with authority and taking charge if it was ignored. Brad would sit on his throne like the king he was. She knew that she would be spending all her free time at the pool so she could be near him.

"I start Monday," Brad said. "I'm the head guard. A couple of other guys will be working under me."

Randy shook his hand as if he'd been burned. "My, my, we *are* the big cheese these days!"

Brad doubled his fist and hit Randy playfully.

11

"And if you show up, knucklehead, I personally intend to duck you!"

That led to a few more cutting remarks, none of which they meant.

The quiet seemed to settle around them. Randy and Tammy wandered off alone, and Lisa could see them, standing under the old oak tree, wrapped in each other's arms. Brad laughed softly.

"Think it will last with those two?"

"Until next school term," she said.

"At least that long," Brad sighed. "But we'll last, won't we, Lisa?"

"Need you ask?"

"You're *my* girl," Brad said firmly. "And that's all there is to it. Even when we go away to college, you'll be my girl, Lisa."

"I *want* to be your girl, Brad. Forever."

"Mmm. Oh, Lisa, it's been a good day and a better night."

"I love it here."

"So do I. But it's getting late. In another ten minutes Tammy will start howling to go home."

"Well, midnight won't wait forever," she sighed.

"Darn it," he said. "How about tomorrow? Let's come back tomorrow."

"I will if I can."

They drove home a few minutes later, leaving the lake behind, Randy and Tammy very quiet in the back seat. Brad dropped them off first and then drove to Lisa's house where a light still burned. Perhaps her father had been called back to the hospital.

Brad kissed her at the door.

"See you tomorrow."

"Goodnight."

She watched him walk away to the car, very tall and straight, confidence written into his every stride. He had hit the homer that had won the state championship, and it showed in his every movement. She was smiling happily when she opened the door and stepped inside.

Her father's medical bag sat on the table just inside the door, so that meant he was home. The television was on, but no one was watching it.

"Hey, what's going on?" she asked.

Her mother appeared, coming into the room in her sure way.

"A million things, dear. Your father had a call from Paris tonight. The seminar has been moved up a couple of weeks."

"Oh, you mean that special work he's going to do over there?"

Then her father came into the room, studying the contents of a manila folder which he popped into an open briefcase.

"You know I'm going over to learn some new surgical procedures, honey. Fortunately I've already put my practice in Doctor Byrd's hands. So I've made reservations for your mother and me. We leave tomorrow night. It means rushing to get things done."

"Mother!" Lisa echoed. "But I thought Mother was going to stay here."

Her parents exchanged a quick look. Her father cleared his throat and gave her his "doctor" look, which meant he was going to be very serious, very firm, and unswayed.

"Your mother decided to come with me, honey," he said. "Our friends, the DeVauxes, have invited us to use their guest room."

Lisa stared at them, her head swimming. "I don't understand any of this."

"We've made arrangements for you to spend the summer in Reynolds with your grandparents," her father said firmly. "They're very anxious to have you."

"What!" Lisa screeched with alarm.

"My parents will love having you, Lisa," her mother was saying. "You'll adore the country in the summertime. I know I did. In fact I still miss it sometimes."

Lisa's head was spinning, and her heart was churning, for suddenly she realized fully what was at stake.

"You mean I have to leave Centerville? You mean I have to spend the whole summer on some stupid farm in Iowa?"

Her father gave her a quick, no-nonsense look. "I'd like to take you with us, Lisa, but the De-Vauxes haven't another spare room. Besides, I'll be spending long hours at the hospital, and your mother has many things she wants to do with her old friend, Jan DeVaux. I really think you'd be bored."

Lisa couldn't quite comprehend it all, couldn't believe what she was hearing.

"But I've got the summer planned — with Brad — I mean."

Her mother's smile was fixed but steady. "Brad won't die without you, dear. Nor you without him."

The tears were burning now, hot and fierce, scalding her eyelids. "You don't like Brad. You've never liked him."

"We've never said that," her father said smoothly. "He's decent enough, I suppose, a little swell-headed, but maybe that comes with being seventeen and the star of the school."

"I *won't* go!" Lisa screamed angrily. "I won't be shipped out to some horrible old farm where there's nothing but cows and chickens and . . . and . . ."

She couldn't finish, for the tears had closed her throat.

"Darling," her mother said gently. "They want you *so* much! They love you. I realize you don't know them very well, but that's another reason I want you to go. You can get to know your grandparents for the sweet, kind, wonderful people they are."

"But Mother — Dad —"

They gave her a sympathetic look and reassured her again how wonderful her summer would be. She knew that she could argue from now until the same time the next day and not dissuade them. They'd made up their minds.

A hollow feeling began to settle in the pit of her stomach. How could she tell Brad? How could she leave him to all the girls that would hang around the pool? How could she spend a summer away from him — the wonderful, beautiful summer they'd planned to have together?

"How could you?" she demanded tearfully. "How could you do this to me?"

Her father put his arms around her for a moment. "Sorry you're so unhappy, baby, but there's no other way. Now think positive. You'll love it more than you think. I know you will, Lisa."

Her mother gave her a wan, hopeful smile. Lisa turned away from them, hating them, her heart filled with dread and remorse. She could almost feel the summer breaking up into tiny pieces under her feet like ice cracking beneath ice skates.

Chapter 2 _____

Lisa couldn't believe it! How could her world have fallen to pieces so quickly? The bus lurched away from the Centerville depot, and with tears burning her eyes she waved goodbye to her friends. Only Jody, who had appeared at the last moment to press a little gift into her hand, seemed to think it was all right. But then Jody would! She didn't know any better.

"I'd love a summer in Iowa like that," she sighed. "But no such luck. I hope you like the book. It's a best-seller."

The bus driver changed gears, the bus began to roll faster, and the faces of her friends disappeared. Lisa's heart turned to lead, and the strange sensation in the pit of her stomach wouldn't leave. It had to be a nightmare!

But the stale smell of the bus was real enough and the feel of the torn cushion of the seat clutching at the denim cloth of her jeans. As they rolled past the last of Centerville and headed to the open highway, she knew it was really happening.

Grandpa and Grandma Maxwell were to meet her at Reynolds, a long seven-hour bus ride away.

"Why a smelly old bus?" Lisa had stormed when she saw that her going was inevitable.

"No trains and no good air connections. It's the best way, dear," her father had said. "Sit back and enjoy the scenery — the time will fly by."

She had tried to get her parents to change their minds and take her with them. If she couldn't stay at home, spending the summer in Paris had to be better than a farm in Iowa any day! But her father was firm about it. He hinted that in addition to the valuable training he was to get, he and her mother would enjoy a kind of second honeymoon.

"I wish I could take you, honey," he had said. "We're going to miss you. We'll phone often. That's a promise. And have a good summer, Lisa. If you put your mind to it, you will."

How could that be? Away from Brad, away from Randy and Tammy, away from all the wild, crazy plans they had made? She had looked forward to long afternoons at the pool, basking in the warmth of the sun, swimming with Brad, the envy of all the other kids, for she and Brad were a special couple.

She hunched down in the seat, closed her eyes, and began the long journey away from her heart.

She tried to read, but the book Jody had given her didn't interest her. With every passing mile she became more apprehensive. Her grandparents were almost strangers! She only saw them at Christmas or sometimes for a special birthday celebration. There were cards and letters and often little gifts for her, but still she didn't really know them.

Lisa solemnly endured the journey, until finally she saw the sign announcing they had arrived on the outskirts of Reynolds. Such a little town! Her heart sank. She had forgotten it was so small. It had been a long time since they had come here to visit, probably ten years.

The air brakes hissed, the bus rolled to a stop, and with her heart thudding, Lisa gathered her things and walked down the narrow aisle, watching her step as she got off the bus.

"Lisa!"

Marge Maxwell was petite, standing barely five feet two. Her hair was cut short and waved naturally, a reddish brown mixed with gray. Suddenly Lisa found herself being enfolded in a pair of loving arms, a smooth, fragrant cheek pressed to hers.

"Ah, Lisa, dear! I'm so glad you've come to us. You don't know how Tom and I are looking forward to this summer. Did you have a good trip? I hope the bus was comfortable. Did your parents get off to Paris all right — oh, listen to me! I'm not giving you a chance to answer, am I? I'm just so glad you've come!"

Embarrassed by this deluge of adoration, Lisa looked about and pulled away from her grandmother. "Where's Grandpa?"

"He couldn't come, and he hated it. But he'll be home for supper, and he's very anxious to see you."

There was a little hassle getting all her luggage. Marge laughed when she saw the amount of it.

"That's all right. But you won't need many things on the farm," she said. "The car's over here. I must stop on the way home at the market. I need a few groceries."

19

Grandma led the way, toting more things than Lisa, talking all the while, laughing happily. Her eyes were a very clear, vivid blue, and they danced with golden lights. Her laughter rang out as easily as breathing, and in a sunback dress her firm, bare arms were tanned a golden brown.

The car was dusty from the country roads. The back seat held a bowling ball and a pair of bowling shoes.

"Our summer league has started," Grandma explained. "Oh, Lisa, I can't remember when I anticipated a summer so much!"

Nothing would do but that Lisa should help her grandmother do the supermarket shopping.

"You must tell me what you like and don't like, dear."

"Don't go to any trouble for me, Grandma," Lisa said stiffly.

Grandma hugged Lisa's arm to her and laughed. "Oh, let me spoil you a little. What are grandmas for?"

Going inside the store was a revelation. For one thing it was not nearly as large as the one they went to at home, and it seemed every aisle they went up or down, Grandma saw someone she knew, either a neighbor from the country or someone in her ceramics or sewing class.

"Tom says I overextend myself," she laughed. "But I enjoy those things. And I have time now. Things are easier on the farm than they used to be. Besides, I'll never get any younger, will I?"

Lisa loved salads, and when she lingered over the fresh vegetables, Grandma shook her head.

"No need to buy those things. Except for lettuce, I raise it all in my garden. I think we've got everything now. It's getting late — supper time."

They left the supermarket, and as Grandma drove the dusty car out of town, she took a road that seemed vaguely familiar to Lisa. Behind them, as Grandma sped along, a cloud of billowing white dust rose up, coating everything as they went.

"It's been very dry so far this year. We need a good soaking rain," Grandma said. "These roads get to be a fright."

A few miles out of town they turned to the left, and this road was narrower but just as dusty. Lisa was conscious of bracing herself. As she recalled, the farm house was nothing very fancy—clean and livable, but nothing like their brick Colonial in Centerville.

Grandma suddenly shoved down the brake pedal and slowed the car. With a laugh she pointed to a straggling flock of chickens that went strutting and squawking across the road in front of her.

"Charlie's going to have to fix the gate on the chicken pens again," she laughed. "They're always getting out."

Slowly Lisa became aware of the old house that sat alongside the road, the chickens heading in that direction. The house had plainly seen better days. Paint peeled and curled, a shutter hung lopsided on an upstairs window, and a shingle or two were missing from the roof. Only the yard was neat and trim, carefully mowed, with a patch of flowers by the front door.

Otherwise, it seemed the place was overrun with

dilapidated vehicles in various conditions, a brood of squealing pink pigs tagging after a grunting old sow, the cackling chickens, a dog, and two cats. Added to all this mixture, she saw at least four young, curious heads turning her way.

The tallest of the bunch, a boy about her own age, with a shock of black, unruly hair, waved to them.

"Hi, there, Marge!"

"Better get your chickens in, Charlie, or they're going to end up on somebody's platter!"

Charlie grinned at that, and Marge drove on. Curiously Lisa turned back to look again.

"Who was *that*?"

"Charlie Shaw. I know the place looks a mess, but they do their best. There isn't a family within fifty miles that I like or respect more."

Lisa swallowed at the dryness of her mouth. She was trying hard not to let the tears surface. She felt so lost here, so alien. The countryside was quiet, the fields of rolling green stretching for miles in all directions, dotted with clumps of trees waving in the breeze. Her hands and face felt coated with the fine dust, and she realized suddenly that she was tired to the bone.

Another mile or so past the Shaw place, they had arrived. Marge turned into the drive, and with a bright smile she gave Lisa a quick glance. "We're here!"

The car bounced to a stop, and a brown-and-white collie came wagging his tail to greet them, staring apprehensively at Lisa but quieting his growl at Marge's soft command.

"Lisa, this is Teddy. We raised him from a pup. Come here, Teddy. This is Lisa."

The dog was the best thing she'd seen so far. His eyes were a warm, gentle brown, and his coat was thick and silky. What a beautiful animal! With a smile Lisa reached out a hand to touch him, and instantly he was brushing against her, quivering with excitement, barking softly as if to say hello. Marge laughed.

"Well, I knew he'd like you. I just knew it! He doesn't take up with everyone like that, you know."

The house stood in the late afternoon sunlight, a tall, two-story building, neatly painted a snowy white and trimmed with green. Flowers were everywhere; their fragrance hung on the air. It seemed to be growing cooler and more moist with every passing minute.

Lisa couldn't begin to take it all in. There was far too much to absorb. First there was the task of carrying in the groceries and all her belongings, Teddy tagging close behind them, overseeing it all.

The kitchen was sparkling clean with modern cabinets, a stainless steel sink, and a round table in front of a window that overlooked the back yard. There was a smell of spices on the air. Something had recently been baked in the oven.

"As a little girl you loved my spice cake," Marge laughed. "I hope you still do."

Marge put away the perishables in the refrigerator and then urged her to come and see her room.

"It's been redone since you were here last. I hope you'll like it."

There was an open stairway from the front hall, and they went up the carpeted steps to another long hall. The last door on the right opened to a spacious corner room. Lisa saw that it had been decorated in pink and white with a huge four-poster bed and a canopy. It was quaint and yet lovely. She couldn't hold back a gasp of surprise.

"You like it!" Marge said, relieved. "Actually, when we redid this room, I had you in mind."

The closet was large enough to hold all she'd brought with her. There was a roomy chest of drawers and a small walnut desk that had been polished to a high shine.

"Your grandfather made this one winter. Keeps him busy. He gets restless when the snow comes and there isn't much to do."

The bath was down the hall, a large room done in powder blue with matching tile and carpeting.

"Your grandfather put a shower in the basement, and he uses that most of the time. He thinks this is too fancy for him!" Marge laughed.

There was no more time for conversation, because there was a loud shout from downstairs.

"Marge, where are you? Have you got our granddaughter up there?"

"Coming, Tom. Come along, Lisa. He's so anxious to see you again."

Lisa followed Marge down the stairs where Tom Maxwell stood waiting for them. He had aged since Lisa had last seen him. There was more white in his hair and deeper lines in his forehead. He was wearing a work shirt and faded jeans with heavy boots on his feet. He was as sun-bronzed as Marge and looked alive and vital. He was a big man, well over six feet with a large frame and bulky shoulders. He laughed with a flashing of his white teeth and reached out his big arms to her. With a shout of greeting he lifted Lisa down the last couple of steps and whirled her around, finally stopping to give her a bearish hug.

"My stars, girl, how you've grown up! A regular young lady now. Where did my little girl go?"

Lisa was embarrassed. They seemed to love her so much! Why did she deserve that?

Dinner, which Grandpa insisted on calling supper, was a bore. The conversation was all about the good corn crop Grandpa had planted and the misfortunes of someone in Grandma's sewing club. Most of all, it seemed Charlie Shaw was the main item of conversation.

"I'll have him down tomorrow to help me with those barn repairs," Grandpa said. "Next to being a good mechanic, he's a pretty good man with a hammer."

Lisa gritted her teeth. How was she going to endure three months of this?

Grandpa gave her a direct look. "You'll like Charlie, Lisa. A real nice boy."

She swallowed hard. Grandma was beaming at her with the same kind of look. Good heavens, were they trying to fix her up with him? She nearly choked at the thought.

"He's got the darnedest biggest watermelon patch you ever saw — but then I'll let him tell you about it. It's his pride and joy."

"Watermelon patch!" Lisa said, crinkling her nose.

"I suppose to a city girl it sounds a little queer to be excited about such a thing," Grandma said with her blue eyes twinkling. "But to Charlie, it's a mighty big operation."

Somehow Lisa endured the meal. Afterwards Grandma thrust a towel in her hands. "I'll wash and you dry."

"I have to do dishes?" Lisa exclaimed.

"I don't have a dishwasher like your mother," she said.

Lisa flushed. Had that been a hurt look in Grandma's eyes? She hadn't meant to sound like *that*, but she had — and she knew it.

"I'll appreciate your help while you're here, Lisa," Grandma said. "Your mother discussed it with me on the phone. A little responsibility never hurt anyone."

Lisa's cheeks burned a bright red.

"On the farm we all have to work together. In fact, the entire neighborhood works together. It's a nice, sound, solid relationship. It gives a person — well — a sense of belonging. I suppose that's as good a way to put it as any."

"But I don't belong here!" Lisa said, flinging down the towel. "I don't."

With that she turned and ran out of the kitchen and straight up the steps to her room. There she slammed the door and flung herself across the bed to have a good cry. All the bitter despair and the disappointment of the empty summer before her came pouring out.

Grandma and Grandpa left her alone. She couldn't have endured their solicitude anyway. Somehow she suspected Grandma understood that.

The next morning the most incredible sound awakened her. She stiffened, listening. Good heavens, was that a rooster crowing? She dimly remembered hearing that before when she'd stayed here as a little girl. She stretched lazily in the comfortable bed. Fresh, sweet air stirred the curtains at the window. Peering out, she saw the rolling hills in the distance and, closer by, the neat, straight rows of young corn, lifting green leaves to the morning sun.

"Lisa!" Grandma called. "Breakfast."

She dressed quickly. How would they act with her? Would there be a scene? Would they be angry or forgiving?

"Lisa," Grandma said, bustling about the kitchen in pair of faded denim shorts and one of Grandpa's old blue shirts knotted around her waist. "Come eat something. Charlie's here."

She came to a surprised halt. Charlie Shaw! The boy from down the road, the one who lived in the old, shabby house and raised watermelons.

"Hey, Lisa," he said, getting to his feet with a grin. He stood a lanky six feet one or two and was so slender, he looked bony. A lock of thick black hair fell to his tanned forehead, and his eyes were a mellow blue with flashes of gold.

"Hi," Lisa murmured.

"Charlie's here to help Tom," Grandma said. "Now you two sit down and have something to eat."

"But Marge, I've already had breakfast," Charlie laughed.

"Never knew you to pass up food," Marge retorted. "Sit!"

Charlie sat.

Lisa stood about dumbly, wondering what she was supposed to say to a boy like this. He gave her a quick, appraising look.

"I hear you're going to stay the summer," he said.

"Yes," she replied.

"Great! You're the prettiest girl I've seen since I don't know when."

Lisa was so surprised by this that for once she couldn't think of a snappy comeback.

"You'll get used to me," Charlie said with a wink. "I say exactly what I think. And listen, you'll like being here. Summer's a great time."

Grandma was serving them a hearty breakfast. Lisa stared at the eggs on her plate.

"But Grandma, I never eat much breakfast."

"Here we eat breakfast. Starts the day off right. Try it, you might like it," she insisted.

Charlie was already eating his with relish. He gave Lisa another grin across the table.

"You know, you've got to meet the rest of our brood. There's three more Shaw kids and Mom. Some of us are nuttier than fruitcakes, but that's okay. Got plans for the future? I bet I can guess."

Lisa found this boy absolutely incredible. Did he ever stop talking?

"Guess," she said with a shrug.

"Modeling, or acting on the stage, maybe some-

28

thing in television doing those commercials for cosmetics. Anything that takes a pretty girl."

She flushed again. His blue eyes were devouring her.

"I want to go to college," Charlie said. "That's step one. Step two — well, maybe philosophy. Teaching. Or maybe I'll do some kind of draftsman work. I've got to wait until I get the right signal, then I'll know it's what I want."

Lisa stared at him. "Signal?"

"Sure," he grinned. "I'll get a message somehow, a gut feeling, a ripple of excitement all up and down me. Then I'll know."

Charlie had finished his eggs and spread jam on a second slice of toast. That seemed to disappear in less than four bites.

"Look, I'd sure like to get to know you, Lisa. But we've got all summer, right? If I don't get a move on right this minute, Tom will come in here after me."

Then abruptly, like the wind moving through the door and then slamming it shut, Charlie was gone.

It wasn't long before they heard the sound of hammering down by the barn. Lisa helped clear the table, and Grandma gave her a pensive look. "About last night —"

"I'm sorry," Lisa said. "I didn't mean to sound nasty."

"It's all right, dear. I know how you felt. It must seem very strange here."

"But I'm not a baby!"

Grandma gave her a quick hug. "No, you're not."

Lisa straightened. "I won't do it again."

Grandma nodded. "Good."

It was after the dishes were done and Lisa had unpacked all her things and put them away that she went downstairs again and outside.

There in the drive was parked the craziest looking automobile she'd ever seen. It had surely been assembled from several different cars, a fender from one, the hood from another, the bumpers from unrelated species, and somehow it had all been put together.

Suddenly Charlie was standing beside her, a broad grin on his face. "Let me introduce you, Lisa. This is The Heap."

"How appropriate," she said wryly.

"It took me several weeks to put it all together and a month to get the engine overhauled and purring like a kitten. Want to take a ride?"

She looked at him with surprise. "No. Thanks!" After Brad's super sports car she wouldn't be caught dead in such a rig!

Charlie shrugged. "I thought you'd like to go to the drive-in movies tonight. I hear it's a good film. A take-off of *Star Wars*."

"No. I don't believe so."

Charlie's blue eyes flickered, and he straightened. "Okay. But I'll ask again. I'd be crazy not to."

"Charlie!" Grandpa was calling.

Charlie sighed and shook his head. "The master calls. Got to scram. I'll give you a raincheck."

From somewhere Grandma materialized, her hands covered with the dark soil of the flower beds, her trowel in hand. "I wish you had accepted his invitation, Lisa. I want you to make friends here. Otherwise I'm afraid you'll be lonely."

"You want me to date Charlie Shaw! Oh, come on, Grandma!"

Grandma didn't say anything, but her smile was winsome. "He's really very nice."

Lisa's temper flared, her nerves jumped, and she faced Grandma with fire in her eyes.

"I have a boyfriend at home. Brad Baker. A really super guy."

"But while you're here —"

"No, thanks!"

Grandma nodded and turned away. Soon she was on her knees weeding in another flower bed, head bent, the sun shining on her head, putting a sheen on the gray that was there.

"Grandma —"

"Yes, Lisa?"

"I'd like to have Brad come and visit while I'm here this summer."

Grandma took a moment to answer. "We'll think about it. Perhaps we can invite him."

If she could have Brad here, even for a weekend, it would make the summer bearable!

Charlie was waving to her from the high rung of the long ladder, shouting something crazy. She didn't want to hear. She would go inside and begin a long letter to Brad.

Chapter 3 _____

Supper was over. Grandpa had retired to the screened-in porch at the rear of the house. It was a comfortable, cozy sort of place with woven throw rugs, easy furniture, and Grandma's plants in hanging pots, mists of green.

Grandpa laughed and rattled the newspaper. "Look at this, Marge. There's an auction sale over around Benton. I think I'll go."

Marge quirked her brows at Lisa. "Oh, dear!"

"Now what's that supposed to mean?" Grandpa asked, pretending to be miffed.

"What on earth will you come home with this time?" Marge wondered. "You should ask him about the prize antique he bought once, Lisa."

Grandpa scowled at them. "Once in a while a man's going to get stung. Maybe I'll find a treasure tomorrow."

Marge's only reply to that was, "Well, we'll see."

"Why don't you two come along?" Grandpa asked. "Lisa, have you ever been to an auction sale?"

"No," she shook her head. "I think I'd rather just stay here, Grandpa."

He flicked a glance at Grandma and then nodded. "Okay, I expect it would be boring. It's a farm sale. Be a lot of machinery and things like that, probably an all-day affair."

The next day Grandpa was off right after breakfast. Lisa helped with the dishes, almost glad to have something to do. It was so quiet here. If it wasn't for her portable radio, which she kept tuned to a rock station, she wasn't sure she could have endured it.

Grandma was out in the yard again, fussing with her flowers. Good heavens, was that *all* she ever did? It would seem so.

"I have bowling tomorrow night," Grandma had told her earlier. "I'd love to have you come along. I know you like to bowl, Lisa."

She remembered the bowling alley at home, the polished, shining lanes, the shouts of her friends, Brad's tall, graceful body throwing a strike or a spare nearly every time. There was the cozy little nook for sandwiches and iced Pepsi. Mostly it was Brad, Randy, and Tammy, clustered together, heads bent close, laughing over private jokes, a clan unto themselves. It was the way she wanted it, the way she loved it. But here . . .

Despair welled up again. How could she endure this all summer long? Nothing to do. Absolutely *nothing*.

"Lisa," Grandma called. "Would you please come and help me? It's going to be hot today. The sooner I can transplant these few flowers, the better."

She was enlisted to draw a pail of water from the pump, to ladle the cool liquid from an old tin cup as Grandma, hands supple and grimy with soil, tended to the plants as if they were the crown jewels. Down on her knees, hair stirring in the wind, she gave Lisa a freckled smile.

"You're such a help, Lisa. This would have taken so much longer if I'd been doing it alone. Thanks so much."

"Sure," Lisa sighed.

Only Teddy made life bearable. The collie tagged constantly at her heels. Grandma, seeing her restlessness, suggested she take a walk.

"Go down by the creek. There are cool willows there — a nice spot for dreaming. I wish I had time for it!"

The creek was a very small trickle of water, not more than four feet wide. But the water was clear, and it bubbled over white rocks on the bottom. The willow branches hung long and cool, and a pretty little white flower grew there, a wild daisy perhaps. And there was still a smattering of purple violets — late bloomers, Grandma had told her, because they were in such a protected area.

Teddy lay close beside her, nose between his paws, blinking sleepily. A bee droned and buzzed by. A cardinal called. Leaves moved in the soft wind. Lisa dropped her head against the trunk of the tree and watched a cloud competing with another in a race across the incredibly blue sky. She ached with loneliness.

"Oh Teddy, if only Brad were here."

"Sorry, I'm not Brad, would I do?"

She was startled to see rangy, loose-jointed Charlie Shaw coming toward her, a battered hat on his head with fishing flies stuck in the band. He plopped down beside her, uninvited. His nose was sunburned, but his grin was wide and friendly. There was a slight chip off one of his front teeth. She saw how smooth and tanned his skin was, and she knew that such a tan would be the envy of all her friends in Centerville.

"Not much luck today," he said, putting his pole aside.

"You mean there are fish in this little stream?"

"Better believe it! What are you doing?"

"Nothing."

He hunched his long legs up under his chin. Then with a toss he flung his hat aside. His hair was thick and black and had a life of its own.

"You know, you ought to have a project," he said.

"What?" she frowned.

He grinned. "A project. The Shaws are all great for projects. Mom's idea. Your Grandma's a little like that, too — always got her hands into something. Now me, I've got The Heap, and I've got my melon patch."

Lisa's stomach curled. What a bore this boy was! Who cared about his crazy melon patch or that awful car?

"You plan just to sit around all summer and do nothing?" Charlie asked.

Her temper flared. "So what if I do? I didn't want to come here in the first place!"

Charlie plucked a blade of grass and began nibbling on it, leaning back on an elbow. "Guess you like it at home," he said.

"I *love* it at home!" she retorted. "This place is enough to drive a sane person crazy!"

He lifted a dark brow at that and gave her another quick grin. "Oh, you'll get used to it. Give it time."

"You make everything sound just great. Well, for your information it's not!"

She got to her feet with a hasty motion.

"Where you going?" Charlie protested. "I didn't mean to scare you away. Hey, if I've poked my nose in where it isn't wanted, I'll amble on. Matter of fact, I've got things to do."

He started to follow her and thought better of it. She walked away, head up, and scarcely glanced back. Halfway to the house she realized she had not been very nice. But what did it matter? Charlie Shaw was nothing to her and never would be!

The day dragged along. Grandma found little things for her to do, but there was no real satisfaction in doing them.

Grandpa came home about two-thirty, the pickup truck rattling noisily up the drive. When he blew the horn, Grandma began to laugh.

"That can mean only one thing. He's bought something, and we're supposed to go and see."

Reluctantly Lisa found herself being urged outside where Grandpa stood grinning all over himself, letting down the endgate of the pickup.

"Couldn't resist this, girls," he said. "I knew Lisa could use it while she's here."

Lisa's eyes widened as a five-speed bicycle, looking to be in excellent condition, came rolling down. "Wheels are important to young folks, I hear," Grandpa said. "Even bikes."

36

He came pushing it toward her, and she gave him a quick, embarrassed look. "Why, thank you, Grandpa!"

"My pleasure," he said. "Now you can chase around and not be holed up here quite so much."

She swallowed at the knot in her throat.

"That's a wonderful thought, Tom," Marge said happily. "It looks very nice. Why don't you try it, Lisa?"

There was nothing to do but climb aboard and shove off. She and Brad used to go biking, up this street and down the next. Oh, what a crazy, wonderful time they'd had! Now she wheeled around the barn lot, spinning about easily, showing her grandparents how well she could ride.

That very evening Lisa took her first long ride away from the house. It would be a godsend! She could go for miles and work off some of her exasperation. As she wheeled along, she realized she was nearing the Shaw place. She looked at it curiously as she passed. There was laughter ringing out from the house, and as she pedaled past she saw a very small boy come racing out the door with an older boy in pursuit. It ended in a flying tackle with the two of them rolling in the grass, laughing and shouting happily until Charlie came to separate them.

"Okay, you guys, Mom's waiting supper. Quit the horsing around and come on."

The little one was snatched up and tucked under Charlie's arm like a sack of potatoes, and the other was collared and pushed ahead of him, all under a playful protest.

It ended in a good-natured scuffle, and watching

them, Lisa was aware of what she had missed being an only child. The screen door slammed, and soon things were quiet around the Shaw place, except for the scratching of the chickens in the dust and the grunting of the pigs. Dusk was falling. Supper was very late at the Shaws. Turning her bike, Lisa rode past again on her way home, wondering about those people who lived there in such splendid camaraderie and total casualness.

The next evening Marge insisted that Lisa accompany her to the bowling alley. "You can bowl yourself if you like," she said. "There's always an empty lane or two. You might meet some young people there."

Anything would be better than staying at the farmhouse!

The bowling alley was larger than she had expected it to be and was filled with women getting ready to spend the evening bowling in their respective leagues. There were introductions to some of Grandma's friends, and Lisa tried to be polite. But she was hating it all!

"I think I'll get something cold to drink, Grandma —"

"Okay," she said. "Wish me luck tonight, Lisa. I'm fourth highest scorer and trying hard for the number three spot!"

The refreshment section of the bowling alley appeared adequate enough. Three young people were huddled in one of the booths, tapping their feet, whispering to themselves, and then roaring with laughter at some unheard joke. Wistfully she thought of Brad and Tammy and Randy at home.

Suddenly one of the boys got up from the booth and came over to her.

"Hi," he said. "You're new around here."

"Yes. Visiting for the summer."

"I'm Kevin Williams, and those two over there are Terry Jackson and Dina Moore. Come on over and meet them."

She soon learned they were the other side of the coin in Reynolds, totally different from Charlie Shaw and more like her friends at home.

"We need another for bowling. How about it, Lisa, want to join us? You and I can pair up, and we'll beat the socks off Terry and Dina," Kevin said.

"Who says?" Terry protested. "You know you can't begin to take me on."

There was a friendly argument, and Dina leaned forward to whisper to Lisa. "Don't pay attention to them. Actually the more they insult each other, the better they like it."

Lisa got along fabulously with them from the very start. Their jokes were sharp and witty; they liked the things she liked. Kevin was the captain of the basketball team, and Dina was a cheerleader.

"Good grief, look at that!" Terry said, scowling. "The entire entourage. You'd think they could go somewhere once in a while without the whole family, down to the littlest one."

It was the Shaw kids! It was the first time Lisa had seen them all at close range. She could pick them out because Grandma had mentioned them several times. The girl was Sue, younger than Lisa, and a few inches shorter than her was Lennie. The smallest of the group was Jonas, a tiny little fellow in a pair of faded jeans and ragged sneakers. Hovering over them all was Charlie, tall and lanky.

"I suppose they all came in that ridiculous car of Charlie's," Dina said.

"I expect he had to stop two or three times on his way here to wire it together again!" Terry said with a smirk.

"Man, if I had to drive something like *that*, I'd walk," Kevin joined in. "He's the town fool, if you must know, Lisa."

She felt the warmth come to her face.

"Oh?" she said, pretending to know nothing about Charlie. "He lives down the road from my grandparents' place, I think."

Sue had drifted away to talk to someone else, and Charlie, with Lennie tagging close behind, had occupied one of the empty bowling lanes.

Charlie was so tall and gangly that when he rolled the ball he seemed all arms, elbows, and legs. All the while he was giving Lennie explicit instructions. When Lennie took his turn, he threw two balls off into the gutter.

Kevin began to get vocal. "Hey, Lennie, which lane you bowling in?"

Lennie flushed and looked over his shoulder, plainly rattled and embarrassed. Charlie said something to him in a low voice.

"Maybe we shouldn't pick on him," Lisa said uneasily.

"Hey, you're not going to side in with those squares, are you?" Dina demanded.

The Shaws seemed somehow out of place in the bowling alley. While Charlie's ball usually rolled straight and true, he wasn't any flashy bowler, just steady. But Lennie wasn't getting any better, and Kevin began to pour it on a little more. They were having a great time at the Shaws' expense when suddenly Lisa realized her grandmother was taking it all in.

"Lisa."

There was a tone in Grandma's voice that put her on guard. She decided it was best to play it cool.

"Oh, hi, Grandma. Do you know my new friends?"

Her quick, bright-eyed gaze swept over them. "I believe they call themselves the Terrible Three. I'm treating the Shaw kids. I want you to join us."

"But Grandma . . ." There was no arguing and Lisa knew it.

The Shaws were already squeezed into the large corner booth. Refreshments had been ordered. Charlie gave her a quick, searching glance, but said nothing. Lennie hunched his shoulders and barely looked at her when Grandma introduced her. Sue gave her a shy smile.

"Gee, you're pretty! I love your hair."

"Thank you, Sue."

"And this is Jonas," Grandma said, ruffling the dark curls of the little boy.

Lisa had never looked into such huge, blue, innocent eyes. He seemed to devour her with one look and then shyly ducked his head away, nestling closer to Marge.

After some of their drinks had been gulped self-consciously, a smattering of conversation broke out, carefully led by Marge. Then abruptly, Charlie pinned Lisa with that direct gaze of his and got straight to the point.

"How long have you known the Terrible Three?"

"I just met them. They seem okay. Don't you think?"

"They're the clique in school. I just thought you'd be — " Then he broke off, shaking his head. "Naw, I should have known."

Somehow, knowing that her new friends were watching every moment of this, Lisa struggled to keep her composure. They surely knew she wasn't enjoying it a bit! She was relieved when Kevin gave her an understanding wink.

At last the refreshments were gone. Charlie said they had to be getting home. They all thanked Marge for the treats, Jonas giving her a shy hug, then turning his huge eyes on Lisa again. She resisted the urge to touch him, to put her hand on his silky nest of hair.

"I've only got one more game to play," Grandma said. "Come join me, won't you, Lisa?"

The game went swiftly, and soon Grandma said goodbye to all her friends. They drove home along the country roads, dust flying behind them.

"Well, here we are," Grandma said, turning down the lane. "Looks like Tom has already gone to bed. He was tired tonight. He works too hard. I know he wanted to finish cultivating the corn in that one big field today."

Car doors slammed, and Grandma led the way inside the house, flipping on the lights as she went.

"I'm for a cool glass of milk, how about you?"

"Sure," Lisa shrugged.

Grandma found a plate of cookies as well, and they sat down at the table together.

"We've had bad seasons lately," Grandma said.

"It gets discouraging. All the hard work and the money it takes to plant a crop these days — but there, I'm boring you."

Lisa couldn't deny it. She frankly didn't understand any of it and didn't want to learn.

"About Lennie Shaw, dear. I think I should explain why I was so upset tonight. You see, Lennie has been very ill lately. It has left him physically weak. Going bowling tonight was a triumph for him. Charlie had promised him a big night bowling the minute the doctor said he could try."

Lisa pushed her glass of milk aside.

"I'm afraid his triumph was spoiled, even if your new friends were jesting, dear," Grandma said gently.

Lisa swallowed hard. "Oh, I didn't know . . . I mean . . . I don't think they realized —"

"I'm sure they didn't, Lisa," Grandma said. She reached out and squeezed Lisa's hand. "I have a rule of thumb. Just be kind to people no matter what the circumstances or temptations are. It somehow always works out better."

The Terrible Three had come down pretty hard on Lennie Shaw. It must have cut deep, it must have spoiled the outing.

"Well, I'm for bed," Grandma yawned. "Busy day tomorrow."

Lisa was elated she'd made new friends, kids who knew where the action was, who saw Charlie as she did. Crazy Charlie, they'd called him. Then her cheeks burned, momentarily. He's been so kind to his brother, she thought, and Lennie hadn't let them get under his skin. She hated the ripple of shame she felt for her part in the matter.

Chapter 4 _____

A warm breeze stirred the curtains at Lisa's upstairs window. She wasn't sleepy at all and lay wide-
eyed, remembering the evening, smiling when she
thought of Kevin Williams. Not that he would ever
replace Brad, but for the summer it would be really
neat to be his friend.

Suddenly the breeze died at the window. She
began to feel hot and uncomfortable. Getting out of
bed, she went to peer out, and she saw that the stars
were hidden now and that a gash of lightning was
rippling across the sky in the north. There was an
oppressiveness in the air, a kind of heaviness that
made it hard to breathe.

Abruptly, as if God had flipped a switch, the
storm began. She had never seen anything come up
so swiftly or with such intensity. The huge trees
around the house began to bend and whip, leaves
lashing fiercely. It took only a moment or two for
her to realize this was no ordinary storm. There was
something wicked and destructive about the wind.

"Lisa! Lisa!" It was Grandma, rapping at her

door. "Come quickly. Get your robe and slippers. Hurry!"

"Where are we going?"

"To the basement!"

Not quite understanding, but sensing the fear in her grandmother's voice, Lisa did as she was told. Before she had reached the door, the lights went out.

"It's all right, dear," Grandma said. "I can find my way in the dark. Tom went down to find the lamp and let Teddy inside."

The thunder was harsh now, the lightning crackling louder than Lisa had ever heard it in her life. She clung to her grandmother's hand.

"First step is right there," Grandma said. "Are you okay, Lisa?"

"Yes," she answered.

Grandma seemed calmer now. She led the way, reassuring Lisa with every step.

"Marge, Lisa! Are you coming?" Grandpa shouted.

He appeared at the bottom of the stairs, an old-fashioned kerosene lamp in his hand. Teddy was next to him, tail between his legs, ears twitching painfully with every crash of thunder and lightning. The wind made the windows sing, and Grandpa took time to go and open a window away from the storm's direction.

"That will let the pressure out of the house," He explained. "Just in case this baby turns into a tornado."

Tornado! Fresh fear rippled over Lisa. She'd seen pictures on television of what a tornado could do, making matchsticks out of houses, twisting trees out by their roots, destroying entire sections of cities. She remembered, too, Dorothy's plight in *The Wizard of Oz*.

"It's always worse in the country," Grandpa was saying. "Nothing much to break the wind these days. Especially here with so many open fields, so few trees."

The basement was cool and damp. The lamp gave the gray walls a yellow glow, and Grandpa set it on a shelf in a safe place. But it didn't reach into the deep, dark corners. It put odd reflections on their faces and glowed against the fruit jars on the shelf beside it. There behind green glass were pickles, jams, and jellies, products of last summer's work. Teddy pressed closer to Lisa, whining softly. She wrapped her fingers in this thick fur and pulled his head against her knee.

"He hates storms," Grandpa said.

"How long do we have to stay down here?" Lisa asked with a shiver.

"Until the worst is over," Grandma answered. "We just feel safer, dear. The wind can be treacherous this time of year."

Grandpa paced about nervously, back and forth, like a caged animal. He talked about the possible damage to his crops and the buildings.

"Don't like it, Marge. Don't like it!"

Marge went to stand beside him, wrapping her arm around him. For no reason Lisa thought of Brad. If he were here beside her, he would be kind and gentle, too, being protective, laughing softly to allay her fears. Later they would remember the night and smile about it.

46

"There went something!" Grandpa said with a start. "Hear it crashing and splintering?"

Grandma clenched her fists, but she kept calm. "Always sounds worse than it is, Tom."

And then, as if that were the finale, the storm blew itself out as abruptly as it had come. It settled down to a steady rain. Grandpa pulled a slicker over his pajamas and went outside for a quick look. When he came back, his eyes were bleak and hollow.

"One corner of the barn is damaged!" he said with despair. "Some of the apple trees are down, but I can't tell about the corn. Sure hope it isn't flattened."

Lisa stifled a yawn, and Grandma insisted she take the lamp and go back to bed.

"We'll be staying up a little while," she said.

Lisa left them talking worriedly about the crops, Grandma hopeful, Grandpa pessimistic.

The morning came bright and clean, rain-washed and fresh. The air smelled different. Breakfast was filled with talk of insurance adjusters, the need of Charlie Shaw's help, and the corn. From the window Lisa could see the young green plants that only yesterday had marched neatly down the field in straight rows, lying now like wounded soldiers.

"Not many broken stalks that I could see," Grandpa said with an air of relief. "It's got a good chance of straightening up."

"You mean it will come back up?" Lisa asked with surprise. "As flat as it is now?"

"With luck," Grandpa nodded. "It's a strong hy-

47

brid, and I've seen it hurt worse than this. We'll pray it does come back up."

Incredible! There were many things she didn't understand about farming and never would.

"You always expect the worst, Tom," Grandma chided.

He gave her a shy grin. "Well, you know it could easily have been the other way. By heaven, I'm sure glad it wasn't."

"We've been lucky again," Grandma said.

Lisa shook her head. They'd suffered considerable damage, and yet they thought they were lucky!

"Lisa, would you do me a favor?" Grandpa was asking. "The phone's out so I can't call. Would you bike down to the Shaw place and ask Charlie to come as soon as he can?"

She swallowed hard. The last thing in the world she wanted to do was face Charlie Shaw this morning!

"Go as soon as you finish breakfast, dear," Grandma said. "I'll take care of the dishes."

"But the road's muddy. I can't ride the bike."

"So it is. Well, maybe you could just walk down."

She tightened her lips and knew what it was pointless to find another excuse.

The rain had come so hard and fast that it had beat the dusty road into a hard surface. Still it made a gummy mess on her sneakers.

She was conscious of her heart thudding as she approached the Shaw house. What must they think of her? What had they said about her last night?

The chickens were strutting in the mud, the pigs were poking their noses into puddles and grunting with contentment. The flowers in the front yard had been flattened by the rain and were mud-speckled.

The back door was open, and through the screen Lisa could hear the babble of voices. They hadn't heard or seen her. For a moment she stood there, feeling like an intruder. There was some excitement about the storm, a few crisp orders from the woman who must be Fran Shaw, mother of this brood, a plaintive plea from Sue. Over it all she was aware that Charlie's voice was the commanding one.

Her rapping stopped every sound in the room. Then Charlie was there, grinning at her, swinging open the door.

"Hi. Come on in. Hey, Mom, this is Lisa!"

Fran Shaw was at the stove, a small, plump woman with a happy face and sparkling eyes. Her hair was brown with sun streaks and cut short.

"Hello, Lisa. I've been hearing all about you."

She flushed. Had they told her, too, about last night? But if they had, it didn't seem to make any difference now.

"What brings you?" Charlie asked. "Did you get hit by the storm?"

"Yes, we did. Grandpa wants to know if you can help him fix the barn. The wind tore it up on one corner."

Charlie shook his head. "That poor barn is fated to die a terrible death! Sure, I'll help him. We were lucky. The wind skipped right over us. I could hear it high up, whistling in the trees. Enough to give a guy goose bumps."

Lennie was avoiding her gaze. When she looked at him, he flushed, and Lisa swallowed hard.

"Goodness, look at the time!" Fran said. "I'll have to rush. I'm going to be late. Now listen, Sue, you take care of the dishes and fix the gate on the henhouse. Lennie, you promised to fix that hog pen — can't have your pigs out in the road again."

"What about me, Mom?" Jonas piped up.

Fram laughed and ruffled his curly hair. "*You* keep out of mischief."

He giggled at that. Then there was a round of kisses and hugs, starting with Jonas. There was something heart-tugging about the Shaws' affection for each other. It made Lisa feel empty. Dad was loving in his own preoccupied way, and maybe Mother would be more so if Lisa didn't shun it. It had always seemed so — so babyish, and yet here, with the Shaw kids, it had seemed perfectly natural.

Fran apologized for rushing off. "I'd like to chat with you, Lisa. Maybe another time, but I've just got to run."

She was out the door. Soon her car started, and she drove away in a decent and halfway respectable sedan, a far cry from Charlie's Heap.

"She works at the grain elevator. She's a book-keeper," Charlie said.

Lisa felt comfortable in the clean but rather shabby kitchen. The furniture was old, and the cupboards needed painting. The linoleum was waxed but showing worn spots. There was no curtain at the window over the kitchen sink, but a frilly white one hung at the other window. Somewhere a rooster was crowing.

"That's stupid old Henry," Lennie spoke up at last. "He's always the last one to crow."

"I guess he's lazy like some of the rest of us," Charlie retorted. "You were the last one up this morning, Lennie."

Lennie shrugged. "I'm just a growing boy."

"Ha!" Charlie said. "A poor excuse is better than none, I suppose."

"You're pretty," Jonas said, having stared at Lisa all this time, seldom looking away from her.

Lisa smiled. "Thank you."

"Where did you get those jeans?" Sue wondered. "I never saw any like those."

"Back home at Davidson's."

"We buy ours at a discount store," Sue sighed. "They're cheaper there. Yours look expensive."

"Davidson's is probably a very exclusive store in Centerville," Charlie said.

"It is," Lisa replied, lifting her chin.

"Figures."

Lisa got up. "I'll tell Grandpa you're coming."

"Give me a couple of seconds to round up some tools, and you can drive back with me."

She would have preferred walking, but Charlie didn't give her any choice. Soon, The Heap was started up, sounding as if it had at least two pistons that weren't working. Clattering and backfiring, the entire body shook as Charlie motioned for her to climb in.

The upholstery didn't match. The seat was green, the back was blue. With a jerk they were off. Lisa was certain they would stall before they had even turned into the road, but Charlie kept manipulating a switch here and a knob there, and soon the motor settled down and began to purr evenly and smoothly.

51

"She's temperamental sometimes," Charlie said, giving her a grin. She saw how white his teeth were and how smoothly tanned his face was. His browned skin made his eyes seem all the bluer and clearer.

"So I see," she said.

"Are you temperamental?" he asked. "I bet you are."

"I suppose you're widely experienced," she said, lacing her words with sarcasm.

"Nope! Don't fool around with the girls very much. I haven't got the time or money."

"Then you're not an authority, are you?"

Charlie swung the wheel of the car to miss a rut in the road and took a deep breath, expelling it from puffed-out cheeks.

"It's like this, Lisa. I know what I like when I see it. You know, there's never been anyone like you in my life before."

She turned a cold smile to him. "But I'm not in your life now."

His brow cocked up, quick and stubborn. "Maybe. Maybe not. I like you, Lisa, even if you have got your nose a couple of notches too high in the air."

"What! How dare you say such a thing? You don't even know me. You know nothing about me, and where do you get off saying a dumb thing like that?"

"Wow!" he laughed. "You've got a temper, too. But sometimes that's a good thing. You can be too quiet, you know."

"What are you, some kind of psychiatrist or something?"

"I read philosophy, and I like to study people — figure out what makes them tick."

"Well, don't bother to study me!"

The moment Charlie brought The Heap to a stop by Grandpa's barn, Lisa climbed out.

"Don't go away mad," Charlie called after her.

She wouldn't dignify that remark with any kind of answer, not even the kind she would have liked to unleash on him!

All day the work went on at the barn, and at lunch time Charlie came in to take his place at the table. The sun had deepened his color, and she saw a burnish of red in his black hair. He and Grandpa had washed up in the basement before coming to the kitchen, and he looked so clean that she expected him to squeak. His blue work shirt was open at the throat, and she saw the deep hollow there, a knotty Adam's apple, all of it giving him a hard, lean look of strength. His eyes were too old for his years, and there was a stubbornness in the way he held his chin; but his gentleness was in the sweet curve of his mouth, which lifted up at the corners in persistent good humor.

For three days, Charlie came early and worked late. He delighted in teasing Lisa, and when Grandma sent her out with a pitcher of cold lemonade, he drank two glasses faster than she could have believed possible.

"Jonas is in love with you," he announced one afternoon while he and Grandpa rested for a while in the shade.

"Jonas is a sweet little boy."

"One thing about Jonas, he knows a good thing

when he sees it," Charlie said boldly. "Learned it from me."

"Honestly, Charlie Shaw, your ego is so inflated it's ridiculous!"

"It's not ego," he protested, "just the truth."

She quickly poured Grandpa the last of the lemonade and went back to the house, and then she decided to go to the creek. Leaving her bike leaning against a tree, she went down to the water and trailed her hands in it, pressing the coolness to her hot cheeks. She had brought a favorite book of poetry with her, and she intended to sit there under the willow, losing herself in its beauty, letting her dreams spill over to Centerville and Brad.

She'd sent three letters to Brad, and he hadn't answered. But then he was busy with his lifeguard job, and no doubt he and Randy and Tammy were filling their spare time with other things. Fun things! Crazy things! Wonderful things! She sighed, realizing how lonely she felt. Empty and floating. No substance. No reality.

She put her head against the trunk of the tree. A circle formed on the water, a hummingbird buzzed by, tiny wings flapping in furious rhythm, his needle beak thrusting itself into the heart of one of the wild flowers in bloom. Then he was gone, off to find another taste of sweetness somewhere else.

She didn't know just when she realized she was being watched. A strange sensation rippled over her skin, and she darted her glance around quickly, not moving her head.

There! Someone moved behind the tree and was hiding there! Her throat closed in momentary fear.

Then she saw a ragged little sneaker and began to smile. It was Jonas!

"Come on out," she said in a low voice. "I know you're there, Jonas."

Finally he crept out into full view. He looked flushed, and his eyes were very round and eager. "What are you doing here?" she asked.

He shrugged his shoulders and gave her a grin that was both shy and happy. "Nothing. Just watching you."

"Why? Don't you know it's not polite to stare at people?"

He scratched the toe of his shoe in the dust. "Okay. I'm sorry."

Lisa seldom came to the creek without something to eat tucked in her pocket. This time it was a package of cookies, and she began to unwrap them. "Have one."

He came closer and finally accepted the cookie. Then, kneeling down by her, facing her, he munched it, never taking his eyes from her.

"What is it with you anyway, Jonas?" she asked.

"Lennie doesn't like you."

"Oh," she said, and a pang of despair went through her, and she wondered why.

"But Charlie does, and Sue thinks you're great. Mom says you're a city girl and must find it funny living here in the sticks."

The cookie was gone, all but a crumb or two that clung to Jonas's lips. "You read those old books all the time," he said.

She realized then that this wasn't the first time Jonas had spied on her.

"Let me read you something. You'll see why."

She found a verse that was her favorite, about a little boy who had died, with his tin soldiers turning to rust. As she read, Jonas grew as still as a mouse and hunched a little closer to her. She realized he hadn't moved for several seconds. Looking down, she saw silky lashes laying against the smooth cheeks and heard his even breathing.

She sat very still, and if a truck hadn't rumbled by noisily over a bridge not too far distant, he might have slept longer. He sat up with a start.

"I've got to go," he said. "Mom will be coming home soon."

Then he was off, tearing through the trees, a streak of sneakers and jeans. Lisa closed the book and put it aside. It had been a strange afternoon. She felt lulled into complacency, as if she couldn't lift her arms or legs. The water trickled along, whispering. The breeze stirred the branches, and for a little while she was locked away in some other strange world where small boys worshipped her, where the sky was the purest of blues, and there was no other time but this moment, no other life, no other heartbeat.

She went home at last, pedaling slowly. Grandpa and Charlie were finishing up, and Charlie was loading his tools into The Heap.

"Hey, Lisa, come look!" he shouted.

She was impressed with the neat job they had done. A professional carpenter couldn't have done it better.

"Farmers have to be jacks-of-all-trades, you know," Grandpa said. "Mechanics, carpenters, conservationists, earth-movers, tilers, even chemists—

modern farming involves a lot of chemicals nowadays."

"You think farming will ever pay a man for all his hours of work?" Charlie wondered aloud.

"Maybe. If people were to go hungry for a couple of weeks, we might be appreciated more."

They took a last look at their work, and Charlie said he had to be going. "Listen, Lisa, you like car racing?"

"Yes," she said.

"Great! There's a race tonight over at Bloomhurst. They've got a good track there, and Larry's driving. You haven't seen anybody race until you've seen Larry. Want to go with me?"

Her heart churned. Grandpa was grinning, liking the idea. He clamped a friendly hand on Charlie's shoulder, and turned, beaming at Lisa.

She swallowed hard. Grandpa wanted her to go. She felt trapped. She knew how much he relied on Charlie for help and how much he appreciated it.

With a deep breath she was astounded to hear herself agreeing. "Okay, Charlie. Yes, I'd like to go."

Chapter 5 _____

The minute the acceptance was out of her mouth, Lisa regretted it. What could she be thinking of! She said something about helping her Grandma in the kitchen and hurried away.

"Pick you up at seven o'clock, Lisa!" Charlie called after her.

Once inside the neat kitchen, she gulped a deep breath, and gave her Grandma a look of despair. "What do you do when you've made a terrible mistake?"

"Sometimes, dear, we can't do anything. But if possible, we try to correct it. What's wrong?"

"Charlie asked me to the races, and I said I'd go. Now I wish —"

"You wish you weren't going," Grandma finished. "I see. Well, I suppose you could phone him and tell him you can't make it. You could make some excuse, but that wouldn't be very honest, would it?"

The phone was ringing, and since Grandma was already setting out things for the evening meal, Lisa went to answer it.

"Lisa!"

Her heart leaped. "Is that you, Dina?"

"Yes. How's things?"

"Lousy," she muttered.

Dina laughed. "I thought it might be. Listen, why don't you join us tonight? Kevin said we'd find something really wild to do. Okay?"

Lisa sighed. "Oh, darn it, Dina. I've got to do something else. Something I don't want to do, but you know my grandparents."

There was an answering groan of sympathy. "Yeah, I know how it can be. Listen, we'll try again, okay?"

"Great!" Lisa said. "I'll be right here, waiting to be rescued!"

Charlie was punctual.

"Hey, Lisa," he said, coming in, with a big grin on his face. "Man, you look really pretty!"

"Thank you," she murmured.

Grandma and Grandpa were beaming at the two of them. Lisa's defensiveness notched a little tighter.

Charlie held the door for her. He stood at least a foot taller than she. He was wearing clean jeans and a plaid sport shirt. He smelled faintly of soap and shampoo mixed in with sun-dried clothes and boot polish.

All the way to Bloomhurst, a town about twenty miles away, he talked about the races and about one driver in particular.

"Larry's one of the best. Fast, but never reckless. He has never had a smash, and he always comes in one of the top three."

The race track was oval-shaped with bleachers

on either side and a pit stop at one end of it where the old beat-up stock cars with numbers painted on their sides were revving up for the race. The time trials were over, and Charlie grinned at the results.

"Just about the way I expected it to be."

Somehow he found them space in the crowded bleachers. She had the most horrifying thought. What if the Terrible Three were here and saw her with Charlie! She searched the bleachers anxiously, but there was no sign of them anywhere. She began to breathe easier.

When the races began, she never heard so much noise. Dust spun from behind the wheels, covering the spectators on the bleachers, and the crowd roared as the race ground on and on. Charlie was on his feet, shouting his encouragement to Larry, his favorite driver.

Larry lost the first race, and Charlie sighed, looking disappointed.

A vendor came through the bleachers selling cold drinks, and Charlie counted out the change for two cans of Pepsi.

The next race was one that awarded a hefty cash prize for the winner.

"Larry's just got to make it this time," Charlie sighed.

The cars started out, gaining speed with every circling of the track. Larry was lagging behind.

"Now, make your move *now*, Larry!" Charlie shouted.

As if Larry had been listening for just that encouragement, his car suddenly shot around the car ahead of him and then overtook a second one.

"Whoopee!" Charlie yelled. "Whoopee!"

Larry was running neck-and-neck with the third car and finally overtook it on the curve.

"That's the way!" Charlie shouted. "That's doing it!"

In his fierce excitement, Charlie gave Lisa a hug. She suddenly found herself held in strong, hard arms, his chin brushing her forehead as he held her tighter and tighter.

Then, with an air of embarrassment, Charlie flushed and let her go. "Sorry. I got carried away."

Larry won the race. Charlie heaved a sigh and grinned at her. "I told you he could do it."

She tried to smile. Strange, he suddenly wasn't just Crazy Charlie any more, but a real live boy with masculine strength and a quick, eager embrace.

Fewer cars ran in the next race, and then there was the last big one. Charlie suddenly seemed very self-conscious.

Lisa stole a look at him. How golden brown his skin was, how smooth his cheek. Even when he had hugged her, his beard had only faintly scratched her. There was a strong muscle tone and sturdy bones. She hadn't realized until now that his lashes were as long and silky as little Jonas's. When he darted a glance at her, their glances locked and held for a long moment, even though the crowd was going wild with what was happening down on the race track.

Larry won that time, too. Everyone began to climb down from the bleachers to go home.

Charlie didn't touch her as they walked back to

The Heap. He held the door for her, but his eyes were veiled, and their glances didn't meet. It was very quiet inside the car, and once they had left the city lights behind, they couldn't seem to think of anything to say. But she was aware of his big, sun-tanned hands on the wheel, the slope of his hard jaw, and the way his hair stirred in the breeze from the open window.

"It's still early. Let's go by Brighton Lake," he said.

She would rather have gone home, but she didn't say so. Why was she being so complacent? Charlie Shaw just couldn't ever be of interest to her. But tonight he seemed — different, and she didn't know what to think about it.

Lisa vaguely remembered the lake from another visit to her grandparents. But she'd forgotten it was so large and that the water looked so black and deep beneath a summer sky. There were several people at the campgrounds. Their fires burned brightly and the aroma of wood smoke drifted on the air.

Charlie took something from the back seat of The Heap and then, taking her hand with a laugh, he drew her away from the car and walked toward the water. Near the edge of the lake, Charlie began to gather twigs and sticks and soon had their own little fire going.

"Marshmallows," he said.

"What?" she laughed.

"I've got to go and cut us some roasting sticks."

He disappeared in the darkness and Lisa sat down beside the little blaze, wondering at this strange boy.

Soon he was back, and the marshmallows had been speared on flimsy sticks. The flames licked the white puffs of sweetness, browning a crust over the melting insides. They feasted on the marshmallows until neither could eat another.

Stars were out, silver buttons popping through the black overcoat of the sky. They were reflected in the lake, and a bird cried somewhere, luring his mate back to the nest. Charlie produced a harmonica from his pocket. He began to play softly, a sweet, sad song that she didn't recognize. The fire burned down, the embers like a red pulse slowly dying away. After a while Charlie stopped playing. He turned toward Lisa, and in the dying light of the fire she saw the sweet curve of his mouth, the laughing look in his eyes.

"A thousand years from now I'll remember this night, Lisa."

She laughed quietly. "Okay, Methuselah, if you say so."

"I do."

He leaned toward her. It seemed right somehow that Charlie kiss her now. His mouth was gentle and kind, sweet. He touched her hair and pulled her head against his shoulder.

The harmonica started again, plaintive, calling to some faraway kindred spirit. Beneath her cheek, Lisa felt Charlie's bony shoulder, noticed the clean, sunshiny smell of him. Her heart ached for no reason she could pinpoint. But she knew that she, too, would remember this moment forever. The cry of the birds, the sound of the lake, the smell of the fire, Charlie playing his harmonica. This special moment was burned into her memory. She reached up and put her fingers into Charlie's black, thick hair. His harmonica skipped a note in surprise but went right on, like Charlie himself. Steady, sure, eager.

"Ah, Lisa," he said. "Lisa."

And for once Charlie didn't elaborate. He didn't need to. For this little time, this one strangely wondrous moment, each knew what the other was feeling. A star fell, streaking across the black sky.

"Make a wish, Lisa. Hurry!" Charlie said.

"I wish —"

For what? She didn't know. She was in limbo. Lost. Disjointed.

"I want this night to never end," Charlie said aloud, just as the star fizzled out and was gone. "Do you think I said it in time?"

Chapter 6 _____

The very next day Lisa took steps to get back on the right track. A phone call to Dina did it, and by afternoon the Terrible Three came roaring out in Kevin's sports car, stirring up dust all the way.

"Swimming!" Kevin announced. "There's no pool in Reynolds, but there is in Bloomhurst. Get your suit, Lisa. We're off!"

"You hit that darned chicken, Kevin. You've got feathers all over your front fender," Terry scowled. "Lisa, have you got a garden hose? We should get this mess off here."

"In the garage," she said.

"That's not the half of it," Kevin scowled. "We darned near went into the ditch because of those little pigs in the road. It's that crazy Shaw place. It looks like something out of hillbilly heaven down there."

"You hit a pig?" Lisa gasped.

"No. Almost," Dina said.

She was relieved. Lennie doted on every one of those little pigs, and they'd miss the chicken.

"If not for eggs, for the stew pot," Charlie had told her once. "We're not a rich family, Lisa. Mom does her best. Dad died when I was just thirteen years old. Jonas was just a baby. But we'll make it. We Shaws stick together, and no matter what anyone says, we'll make it, one way or another!"

She remembered Charlie's fierce determination, the glint in his eyes as he said that, and she heard the pride ringing loud and clear.

The boys made short work of the chicken feathers with the garden hose, and they all drove away a few minutes later, leaving the pile of feathers on Grandma's drive.

The Bloomhurst pool was busy, and the minute Lisa appeared with her new friends, she saw the glances come their way. Everyone was shouting to either Kevin or Terry. Lisa began to smile. Why they were just like Randy, Tammy, and Brad at home! The golden ones. The "ins" of the school kids. How could she have been so lucky!

"Kevin won the swimming meet last year," Dina told her. "And he's probably going to get a college scholarship at Ohio State. The football scouts are already watching him. They're ranked very high, you know."

"I know!"

Dina spread suntan lotion on her legs and gave her a direct look. "There's somebody at home, isn't there?"

"I've told you about Brad. Kevin reminds me of him. They don't look alike, but they're both star athletes, very special."

"Hmm." Dina smiled. "You know Kevin's got a steady girl."

Lisa tried to keep her smile bright and saucy. "Oh?"

"But she's away for the summer. They've got this arrangement. He can date while she's away, and she'll do the same thing. A very sensible thing to do, don't you think?"

"Oh, yes! Well, that puts us in the same boat, doesn't it?"

"That's why he likes you — and goodness, Lisa, you *are* a knockout."

"Look who's talking," Lisa laughed.

Dina gave her shoulder a shrug. "Listen, I've found this wonderful salon. If you need a haircut or anything while you're here, let me know. I'll fix you up."

They talked like this off and on all afternoon. Kevin showed her all his fancy dives and challenged her to a race. He won by only three strokes, and he lifted a brow with surprise.

"Hey, you're good!" he said.

"I told you so," she retorted.

And then he kissed her. Lightly, in fun, but it was just right. No strings attached, it said, but at the same time it marked her as his summer date. She knew that half the kids at the pool saw it. And they understood! Just as they understood at home that she and Brad were a couple. That they were a world unto themselves and intended to keep it that way.

She hated to see the afternoon end. But it did, and when they dropped her off at the house, they promised to come back again soon.

At the supper table that night there were several questions about what she'd done. Grandma was being polite, nice. Grandpa scowled and said little. He didn't approve of her new friends. It didn't surprise her. Mother and Dad didn't appreciate Brad either. How could someone as old as her grandparents even begin to understand about Kevin Williams and her other new friends?

Charlie crossed her mind. She didn't want to think about him, but he kept crowding her thoughts at odd times. What on earth was she doing, getting involved with two boys while she was here this summer? Anyway, her heart was really at home with Brad.

The next day, Brad's first letter finally arrived. It was very short and told her almost nothing. It wasn't the kind of letter she had expected or hoped for. He said he was very busy with his lifeguard job and Tammy and Randy sent their best. He didn't reply to her invitation to visit. He signed it, "Love," but he didn't *say* he loved her. And she had crowded nearly every line of her letters with that precious word!

She thought to herself, "Everything's so mixed up."

But she began to worry too. Perhaps, like Kevin, Brad had found a new summertime girl to take her place while she was away!

With that disturbing thought on her mind, she was almost relieved to hear about the summer job Grandpa knew about.

"Walking the beans?" she asked. "What is that?"

"Marge and I usually do it ourselves in our fields, but there are crews that can be hired to do it. Some of the farmers hire kids to walk the soybean fields.

They chop out the extra corn and the button weeds."

"But why?"

"We don't want the trash in the beans when we're harvesting them. Foreign material means a dock in price too when you sell. We want the bean fields clean for a clean harvest. Simple as that."

The Shaw kids were signing up for the work and Sue invited Lisa to join them. At first, she wasn't sure she wanted to, even though it was a way to spend the slow-moving days. Then she learned the Terrible Three were going to be part of the crew as well. Dina told her about it on the phone.

"It's a great way to get a tan and make some extra money. Which I could use! Terry's signing up too and if Kevin finds out you're interested —"

"Oh!" Lisa said with a gasp of pleasure. "If you're all going to be there —"

"Then you'll do it?"

"Yes," she laughed. "I'll be there!"

When Lisa sprang this news on her grandparents, they were surprised, to say the least.

"I'm glad you've decided to try it," Grandpa said. "It's good money, and the farmers really need the crew to help out. I'll sign up with Whitlock to have our fields done, too."

"I'm certainly glad to hear *that*!" Grandma laughed. "I wasn't looking forward to the job at all. It's for the younger ones."

Lisa still wasn't sure she liked the idea, but if the Terrible Three were going to be a part of it, wild horses couldn't keep her home.

The next day Lisa rode into town with the Shaws to sign up for the crew. Charlie, Lennie, and Sue were all anxious for the work. But they were disappointed when they learned that Mr. Whitlock was offering a dollar less an hour than they'd received last year.

Charlie sighed. "That's a hard nail to bite."

"Can't be helped," Whitlock said. "It costs the farmer too much to hire us. I had to scrounge to get enough fields to run the crews this year. Frankly, an airplane can spray and do the job more cheaply than we can. I doubt I'll run my crew at all next year."

"Well," Charlie said, "all good things come to an end eventually, don't they?"

"It's still good money," Sue persisted. "And we can't pass up the chance." She turned to Lisa. "I'll fix a thermos jug of ice water. I'll share it with you, Lisa. Wear a hat. And you'll need sunglasses, too. It's hot and bright out there."

The next morning the alarm went off before six. With a groan Lisa burrowed sleepily into her pillow. But Grandma was pounding at the door.

"Breakfast in ten minutes, Lisa. Better dress now. It will soon be time to go."

What had she gotten herself into? She asked herself that while she was washing her face and brushing her teeth. Then, after putting on a halter and shorts, she went down the stairs.

Breakfast was always huge at Grandma's table. Grandma kept urging her to eat.

"It will seem like a long time until noon. I've packed you a lunch."

Grandma produced a wide-brimmed sun hat and insisted she take a blouse with her.

"Just in case the sun is too warm. Watch out you don't burn."

She heard The Heap coming in the drive, and snatching up her belongings, she rushed out to meet them. Charlie gave her a grin. Dressed in a faded shirt and cut-off jeans, he looked lankier than ever. Sue was attired in much the same fashion. Lennie wasn't wearing shorts, but his jeans had tears at the knees and a pocket torn off the back.

"Pile in," Charlie called. "We're running a couple of minutes late."

There were two crews, six in each with one person in charge. Charlie was quickly appointed to that job, and Dick, another boy, was selected for the other crew. Lisa made certain she was in the same group as the Terrible Three, but none of them were happy when they learned Charlie would be their foreman.

Hoes and long-handled hooks, sharpened to a razor's edge, were passed out. Then they were all loaded into an open truck and driven out of town to one of the many fields they were to see in the next couple of weeks.

It was huge! Lisa could see green rows of soybeans stretching across the field into eternity!

"It must be a mile to the end," she gasped.

"This is a hundred-and-twenty-acre field," Charlie told her. "There's a hundred and six square rods to an acre. Or two hundred and eight feet, eight and a half square inches to the acre. You figure it out."

"Okay, wise guy," Kevin said in a cocky voice. "How far is it anyway?"

Charlie gave Kevin a quick look, and a dull flush came to his cheeks. Lisa caught her breath. She'd never seen Charlie lose his cool. Finally he relaxed and managed a grin.

"Before the day's done, you'll say it's too far."

With that, Charlie put them to work. Growing between the soybean plants, the green corn shot up with sharp leaves, and weeds were determined to take root. Charlie taught Lisa how to use the hoe, cutting out the unwanted growth.

"Don't worry about between the rows. The farmer can get all of that with the cultivator."

"Cultivator?"

"It's like a plow," Charlie answered. "You must have seen one at your Grandpa's place."

She flushed, feeling very dumb. Then Charlie grinned. "It's okay. Lisa. I guess everything's new to you."

Kevin had been watching Charlie pay attention to her, and he didn't like it. He came edging closer, leaving some of the plants in his rows uncut. All in all, Kevin was doing a halfhearted, sloppy job.

Charlie didn't miss any of it and made Kevin backtrack.

"Ah, heck, what's a weed or two anyway?" Kevin argued.

"We're here to get them *all*," Charlie replied. "If you don't want to do it the way I tell you, then turn in your hoe."

"You'd like that, wouldn't you?" Kevin said. "You think you're some kind of hotshot, don't you?"

Lisa saw Charlie double his fist.

72

"Don't, Charlie," Lisa said.

"Oh, come on, Kevin, and do your job right," Dina shouted. "It's a long way to the end, and I'm thirsty already."

Kevin chopped the leftover weeds while Charlie stood over him and then grudgingly took his place alongside the others. Charlie looked as if his smile had turned to stone. So he *could* be rattled, Lisa thought! There were times she thought he was far too goody-goody. Somehow, knowing that he was human and could get angry like everyone else made her like him more.

At first Lisa thought the job might be fun. Everyone shouted back and forth, and complained their rows had more weeds than anyone else's. It went like that across the field and back, until soon Lisa began to feel as if her arms were going to swing out of their sockets. Her legs ached, her shoes were dusty and soiled, the dry clods of the rough earth made it hard to walk. Her throat was so parched, she thought she'd die before they stopped for a rest and a cool drink of water.

Sue shared her thermos of iced water with all of them. When Kevin finished drinking all but a little from the cup, he tossed the rest at Sue, making her shriek with surprise. Then, embarrassed and flustered, she flushed furiously. She stumbled away to hide her confusion.

"Poor clod," Kevin smirked. "She's lumpy in all the wrong places."

Charlie suddenly appeared and put a warning hand on Kevin's shoulder. "One more smart remark about any of my family, Kevin, and you're off my crew. Got it?"

Kevin shook his hand free, and Lisa feared a fight would break out in earnest this time.

"You know what you can do with this damned job?" Kevin asked through clenched teeth, tossing his hoe down at Charlie's feet.

"Fine with me. I figured you wouldn't stick."

With that Charlie walked away. Kevin's face was far too red, and his shoulders were hunched in fury.

"Going to let him get the best of you *again*?" Terry asked in a quiet voice.

Kevin sulked for a moment, and then with a cold smile he picked up his hoe.

"No, I'm not, Terry. I'll show him!"

Lisa's head began to ache after all the commotion, along with the dizzying effect of the broiling sun. Chop, chop, chop. Another weed bit the dust. A green cornstalk fell like a wounded soldier into the row. Walk, walk, walk. Chop, chop, chop. Throat parched. Face reddening with heat. Legs like hundred-pound weights. Feet aching. Shoulders with burned-out sockets, bones brittle with fatigue.

Noon at last! They were trucked back to the city park in Reynolds where everyone ran for the water faucets, letting the cool water pour over tired hands and arms, bathing their faces.

Under leafy shade trees they devoured their lunches and caught a few winks of sleep, too tired to argue about much of anything, thinking only of the day's end.

Only the Shaw kids seemed unaffected. Full of energy, they were laughing among themselves, scuffling good-naturedly as if they worked like this every day!

74

Kevin stretched out and put his head in Lisa's lap. She looked down into his eyes, and he smiled. His anger had cooled, and he was pointedly ignoring all the Shaw kids.

"Let's quit," he said in a whisper. "Let's just slip away and let the others go back to the fields if they want. We could find something special to do."

There was no chance to answer, for Charlie was clapping his hands and calling to them.

"Everyone back in the truck. Time to go back to work."

Everyone groaned again. Kevin was the last to get to his feet. It was Lennie this time that gave him a cold smile.

"What's the matter? Too soft to make it?" Lennie asked.

Black anger crossed Kevin's face, and Lisa quickly took his arm and tugged him away.

"Come on, Kevin. Let it go."

They worked until two-thirty, all but melting in the hot sun. When they reached the end of their rows, Charlie called it quits for the day, and they were driven back to town.

"It's too hot out there," Whitlock agreed. "Be here at seven tomorrow morning."

Kevin insisted he wanted to take Lisa home, and she went with him, aware that Charlie was watching her every move, his eyes flickering. Two spots of red showed in his cheeks. She looked away quickly. He felt defeated, seeing that Kevin had won. Why should she feel guilty, she asked herself?

For two weeks they battled the bean fields, and Grandpa's place was the last one.

There were three days of walking to be done there, and on the afternoon they were to finish, Grandma decided to throw a party.

"All of you have worked so hard, I thought a picnic might be fun. Invite them all to come, Lisa."

It was about five o'clock in the afternoon when they reached the end of the last rows.

"Whoopee!" Charlie shouted. "We've finished. Whoopee!"

Everyone took up the chant, and Lisa shouted for them to remember the picnic.

Going back to the trucks for the ride to the house, Kevin and Terry were in a huddle. Dina gave Lisa a tired grin.

"At least we got a terrific tan, and I made enough money to buy some really classy clothes for school. What about you? Think it was worth it?" Dina asked.

"I suppose so. At least it's two weeks gone out of the summer."

In a way Lisa had enjoyed it. But more than anything, she enjoyed the fact that she had become quite good at the job. She found she could chop and walk as fast as the Shaw kids. She worked right beside them, keeping pace while the others had consistently fallen behind. She had always finished her rows long before they had.

Grandma, with Grandpa's help, had set up some tables under the trees in the back yard. All kinds of food waited for them, including pitchers of iced lemonade and a tub of soft drinks. Mounds of sandwiches, potato salad, baked beans, fresh bread,

76

chips, olives, pickles — there wasn't anything missing.

"Listen, Lisa, could I speak with you?" Kevin lured her away from the others and smiled down at her. "Listen, let's split. This isn't our cup of tea."

Lisa's mouth sagged open. "You mean you don't want to stay for Grandma's picnic?"

Dina and Terry had joined them. "We've heard about this fabulous disco. A new place. It's their opening night. We thought we'd check it out."

They were dead serious! It sounded super, and Lisa was tempted. "I can't go. You know this is my house, sort of my party."

Kevin scowled. "Really, Lisa, can't you duck out? I mean —"

"Maybe later."

"It's now or never," Kevin said evenly. "How about it? Come on, sweetheart."

She felt tears burning her eyes. "I just can't."

"Okay!" Kevin said angrily. "Okay. Forget it. Gang, are you ready to split?"

They left five minutes later, barely saying goodbye to anyone. A sinking, hollow feeling came to Lisa's stomach. Why couldn't they understand?

Back home she and Brad had done things like this, and it had seemed okay. Queer, she'd never looked at it in just this light before.

"Lisa." Grandma was standing beside her. "I guess your new friends had other plans. I'm sorry it interfered with the picnic." Her eyes smiled at her.

"So am I!" Lisa sighed.

Grandma linked her arm with hers. "There's one

thing, honey," Grandma said. "Even though we bleed and suffer for the wrong things our friends do as well as delight in the right things, we're not liable for their actions. So don't worry about the Terrible Three. You're only responsible for yourself and what *you* do."

Chapter 7 ──────────────

The party was spoiled for Lisa. But the others didn't seem to notice or even care that the Terrible Three had gone. They stayed and stayed, laughing and calling to each other, engaging in all kinds of horseplay.

At the end of the party, Charlie said, "I've been neglecting my melon patch. I've got to get out there and get after the weeds."

Once Charlie had insisted Lisa see it, and she had gone out there with him. He had examined the vines for blight or insects, and there, nestled in the wide green leaves amid yellow blossoms, lay little green nuggets.

"Melons just setting on." Charlie grinned proudly. "I like the dark green round ones the best. But I grow several varieties."

From time to time Charlie had told her in detail about the patch and how the crop was developing. Like Grandpa, he worried about their needing rain or if they'd had too much, and she found it a little bizzare that anyone could absolutely flip over a melon patch!

She knew, though, that the melons were progressing nicely and that Charlie was pleased.

"He's got reason to be proud," Grandpa said. "He's really done a good job, and he's worked like a maniac."

"Like you," Lisa replied.

Grandpa smiled at that. He was often up before the sun and didn't stop working until well into the evening. "It's the life of a farmer," he said. "The only lull we have is in August when the corn is getting tall and the cultivating is all done and the beans are walked. But then it's time to paint the buildings or make repairs, fix fences. And weeds. It seems like there are always weeds to get rid of. Then with September it's time to get the harvesting equipment ready to roll."

"Don't you ever stop, Grandpa?"

"Truthfully, winters are pretty easy these days. Unless you raise stock. But since I don't have much, I'm a free bird for a couple of months, anyway."

Grandpa was feeling a real glow these days. He went around with a smile on his face, for his crops looked very good.

"If we don't get hail or wind or if it doesn't turn off dry, I think we might do better than usual."

"Is that all you think about, Grandpa?" Lisa asked with a frown. "The bad things that can happen?"

"Nope. But a farmer has to think about such things. He goes out there with a few seeds and a planter, works the soil, plants the seeds, then prays for rain. He puts his trust in the Almighty."

Grandma was deep into her bowling league activities, and there were tournaments going on now. "I'd like for you to come, Lisa. You, too, Tom."

Grandpa grinned. "Might come and watch if I won't make you nervous, Marge."

"I need moral support from both of you. Do you know, if we win this tournament, we go to the state meets? That'll mean three or four days in Des Moines!"

Several days had slipped by since the party, and Lisa had not seen nor heard from the Terrible Three. But the bowling alley was one of their hangouts, and since Grandma wanted her to attend the tournament games, it seemed like a golden opportunity to see them again.

The bowling alley that night was crowded and noisy. Grandma gave her a hug. "Wish me luck?"

The minute she could, Lisa slipped away and took a quick look around.

"Lisa!"

Her heart skipped a beat. Kevin was motioning to her, and with a smile she went to join the Terrible Three in their favorite booth where they were munching on pizza.

"Listen, you really missed a good time at the disco."

"I'm sorry," Lisa said. "I really was in a bind, you guys. You must *know* that."

"Sure," Dina said with a wink. "But we just couldn't pass it up. You know how it is."

She laughed. She did know. She and Brad would have done the very same thing. She began to relax and enjoy herself. They weren't angry with her! They seemed to have brushed aside all their misunderstanding. She was certain of it when they made plans for Saturday night and included her.

The night of bowling ended at last with a loud, noisy cheer. Grandma's team had done it! They were headed for Des Moines.

"I can't believe it," Grandma said, eyes shining. "Did you see that strike that Emma threw?"

"Come down off the clouds," Grandpa chided. "Okay, I'll take you to supper tomorrow night to celebrate. How about the Inn over at Bloomhurst?"

"Tom, that's so expensive!"

"Only the best will do for you, Marge."

Lisa was caught up in their happiness, because she felt happy, too. She was back in the good graces of the Terrible Three. Until now she hadn't realized how much that mattered.

Then Grandma sprang another surprise. "Lisa, why don't you come to Des Moines with me? We won't be bowling all the time! We can go shopping, have lunch in some nice place, and there's surely a pool at the motel. We could have a kind of holiday!"

The idea intrigued Lisa. It might even be fun! Maybe she could find some fabulous new clothes for school. Excitedly, the two of them began to plan the trip. Grandma was more keyed up than Lisa had ever seen her. They were to leave early Friday morning, and all day Thursday Grandma fussed about packing her things. She'd splurged on a new outfit and modeled it for Lisa, acting as happy and young as a teenager.

"I guess I must seem a little silly," Grandma laughed, "being so excited about going to Des Moines."

Lisa shrugged. "It's your thing to enjoy, Grandma."

Just then the phone rang. "One of the girls checking on something, I expect," Grandma said, hurrying to answer it.

Then Lisa saw the way her grandmother straightened and gripped the phone tighter. "This *is* Marge. Charlie, what on earth is it? You sound so strange . . ."

There was a pause, and Lisa knew something was very wrong.

"Oh, my goodness! How awful," Marge gasped.

In a moment, she spoke again, reassuring him. "I'll be down first thing in the morning. You kids aren't to worry about a thing."

At last, Marge hung up.

"It's Fran Shaw and Sue. They've been in an auto accident. Charlie says everything's under control now, but Fran won't be home for several days. Sue fared a little better. A broken arm, but with a cast she's not going to be able to take care of that family."

Lisa's eyes widened. "You mean you're going to take over?"

"Of course. They need my help."

"But Grandma, you can't go down there and take care of the Shaws!"

"Why on earth not?"

"Your bowling tournament! Des Moines, our big trip."

Grandma took a deep breath. "Elsie Williams can sub for me. She's very good and will jump at the chance to go."

"But Grandma! You want to go, you've been *dying* to go."

Grandma took a deep breath. "I couldn't go and enjoy myself, knowing that good friends needed me. I'm sorry if you're disappointed."

"But Grandma —"

"Might as well save your breath, Lisa," Grandpa spoke up. "I've lived with this woman too long. She's got her head set, and she'll not change her mind."

Lisa was angry. "I don't think it's fair, Grandma! I think you're crazy if you let your tournament go by."

"I just can't be that selfish, Lisa."

The matter was settled. Lisa could see that. She was angry and disappointed. It was all so unnecessary!

The worst came the next morning. After breakfast, Grandma was off and on her way to the Shaw house. She left explicit instructions for Lisa.

"Sue may possibly get home today. If so, I may spend the nights there for a little while, just to see that all goes well. I'm putting you in charge of the house, Lisa."

Lisa gasped at being saddled with that responsibility. "But Grandma —"

"Your grandfather will be out most of the time. And he's got a business meeting in town tonight. It's up to you to keep things going smoothly. You know about everything — and I trust you, Lisa."

"Grandma!"

"Please stay close to the phone. Just in case I need you."

"I have to stay inside!?"

"Please," Grandma said, with a nod of her head.

Lisa tried to argue the point, but she might as well have talked to a stone wall! Grandma took the car and drove away. There were dishes to do. The laundry had piled up. The house needed dusting, and the vacuum sweeper should be run. Grandpa would have to have lunch!

Lisa took her anger out on the work at hand, whizzing through it in a sloppy way. Well, it would have to do! What did she know about cooking? And Grandpa always expected meat and potatoes on the table — a farmer's meal — and she knew from zero about such things!

In the middle of the morning she looked up to suddenly find Jonas in the house. "What are you doing here?" she asked crossly.

Jonas blinked. "Marge said I could come if I wanted to."

Now she was going to be a baby-sitter! Great! Just great!

"Mom's real sick," Jonas said, his eyes as huge as saucers.

Lisa took a deep breath. She realized she hadn't even bothered to ask how she was. She softened a little. "I'm sorry, Jonas. I really am."

"Are you mad at me?"

Lisa drew a shaky breath. "No. I'm just mad at . . . at . . . everything, but not you, Jonas."

He grinned, and his cherub look touched her heart despite herself. "Read me a story," he said. "Please?"

He held out a grubby little book she knew was

his favorite. With an air of resignation she took it. "Oh, okay! But just one. I've got too many darned things to do around here!"

"Oh."

"And I hate it," she shouted at no one in particular. "I hate it!"

Chapter 8 _____

Things didn't get any better. As far as Lisa was concerned, they got worse. Grandma was off every morning the instant breakfast was over, leaving Lisa with the table to clear and the dishes to do. On top of that there seemed to always be a dozen other things that needed to be done.

"How long will you have to be at the Shaws?" Lisa asked angrily.

"Goodness, there's more work down there than two women can handle. I know Sue does her best, but with Fran away all the time things have been neglected. The house needs a thorough cleaning from top to bottom."

"Must *you* do it?" Lisa asked.

"I want to, dear. Sue's not going to be able to do very much with that broken arm, you know."

Sue had come home from the hospital the day after the accident. Fran, though, had no hopes of being discharged for a couple of weeks. Grandma seemed obsessed with doing all she could for them, and Lisa was stuck.

It irked her bitterly. Resentfully she did what she

had to do, feeling more rebellious every day. It was on one of those particularly low days that she heard someone blowing a horn. Rushing to the window, she peered out.

"The Terrible Three!" She laughed happily. She ran out to meet them, and they were bubbling over with plans.

"Come along with us, Lisa. We've got a great day planned. We'll have lunch at a taco place I know," Kevin said. "And we'll drive around for a while and see where the action is. Later maybe we can go discoing or swimming — we'll find something to do."

"Oh, that sounds great."

"Well, then, let's go!" Kevin insisted.

She looked back at the house. Grandpa was out in the field, mowing weeds along the fence rows. He would be home expecting lunch soon.

"I can't," she said. "I have to stay here!"

"Dullsville!" Dina sighed. "Why do you have to stay?"

She explained that her grandmother was away and that she was supposed to look after things in her absence.

"Can't a man as old as your grandfather fix his own lunch?"

Lisa hesitated. Grandma was adamant about Grandpa having a hot meal at noon.

"Come on, doll," Kevin coaxed. "Can't you just leave a note or something?'"

She took a deep breath. Why should she have to stay and mind the house? Why should she be cheated out of the few good times to be had here?

"I will!" she decided. "I will!"

With a defiant air she went back to the house, scrawled a note, and left it on the kitchen table. Then, with a laugh, she climbed in beside Kevin. He flashed her a cute grin.

"You know, Lisa, I'm sure glad you came to Reynolds."

They spun away from the house, and Kevin turned the car toward town.

"What if Grandma sees me when we drive by the Shaws?"

"Hunch down," Kevin laughed. "Go on!"

Giggling, feeling silly and a little guilty, Lisa did so as Kevin went tearing by the Shaw house, raising dust as he went.

"Hey, what's that?" Kevin asked, suddenly slamming on the brakes and shoving the car into reverse.

"Oh, that's Charlie's watermelon patch," Lisa shrugged. "You'd think he was raising diamonds out there instead of melons."

"There must be millions of melons!" Dina gasped.

Kevin laughed as he got out of the car, quickly climbed over the fence, and went trodding into Charlie's melon patch. In a few moments he came back grinning.

"Won't be long until they'll be ripe. Hey, Terry, maybe we should have a watermelon bust one of these nights."

"Yeah!" Terry laughed. "We'll invite everybody."

Lisa swallowed hard, feeling vaguely uncomfortable. She wasn't certain what they were planning. Probably just some impish fun.

"Crazy Charlie!" Kevin was scoffing. "What won't he do next? *Melons,* for crying out loud."

Lisa was glad when they drove on. She didn't want to think about Charlie or any of the Shaws or of Fran lying in the hospital struggling to get well so she could come back to her brood. She especially didn't want to think about Grandma or the fact that she'd gone against her instructions. Lisa lifted her head. What did she care anyway? She was anxious to have a good time for a change. And a good time they had! The Terrible Three, which Kevin redubbed the Fabulous Four because Lisa was along, knew how to make things happen. All in all, it was about eight o'clock before they took Lisa home. As they drove up to the house, she saw the lights burning inside. She swallowed hard. Grandma had come home.

"Hey, take it easy," Kevin said. "You okay?"

"Sure," Lisa replied. "I can hold my own with Grandma!"

Famous last words! She waved goodbye to everyone, and Kevin kissed her before she climbed out of the car and went to the door. She waited until they had driven away before she went inside.

Grandma was in the kitchen, doing dishes. She looked up for a moment, saying nothing.

"Hi," Lisa said.

She tried to go right past her, up to her room, but Grandma stopped her.

"Where have you been, Lisa?" Grandma asked.

"Out," she said airily. "With my friends. Is there a law against that?"

"No. But you left such a vague note. We didn't know where you were. We guessed you were with Kevin Williams, but we weren't sure."

"Yes, I was, and I had a great day. It's about time I had a little fun around here."

Grandma hung the towel neatly on the rack. "Meaning that you don't usually enjoy yourself?"

"I didn't expect to have to look after the entire place! I don't think it's fair to shove that off on me, Grandma!"

"I see."

"Now I think I'll go and do my hair."

"I'm not finished yet," Grandma said firmly. "We pull as a family unit around here. We all work together, and we play together. We share the responsibility. If you had phoned me it would have been different. As it is, Lisa, you acted very irresponsibly!"

"No!" she retorted. "I acted like any girl that wants to go out and have a little fun in her life! What do you want me to do, just sit here and die of loneliness?"

Grandma's eyes flickered, and she sighed. "I didn't realize you felt so bitter, Lisa."

Lisa swallowed hard, but couldn't think of anything to say. Grandma looked so weary.

"Lisa, you're going to learn that you can't just go off and do what you want all the time. Life doesn't go that way. It would be nice if it did."

"If the sermon's over," she said icily, "I'll go to my room now!"

"I want you to promise me that you won't do this again without our permission. We left the house in

91

your charge, Lisa, and you turned your back on it."

"Nothing awful happened, did it?" she asked quickly, hotly. "It didn't burn down or anything."

Grandma's lips tightened. "No. But Grandpa had little for lunch, and he missed an important phone call that necessitated his making a drive to Cartersville that was pointless and useless. It took valuable time."

"Well, I'm sorry. I wasn't told there was going to be a phone call. And there was plenty of food in the refrigerator for Grandpa!"

With that Lisa turned on her heel and stalked away. Grandma let her go. Going into her room, Lisa slammed the door shut. Tears were perilously close.

She had trouble falling asleep that night, but at last she dropped off. It seemed only minutes later that she dimly heard a phone ringing somewhere.

"Dear, get up! It's your mother and father on the line from Paris!" Grandma called.

Lisa quickly shook the sleep out of her eyes, snatched up her robe, and hurried downstairs. Grandma and Grandpa had already talked with them, and they handed her the phone.

"Lisa! Hello, dear."

"Mother, is that you?"

"Yes. Yes!" came a familiar voice from far away. "How are you, darling?"

"I can't hear you very well," Lisa replied.

"I can't hear you either! Speak up, dear."

The connection was very noisy, but they managed a conversation by shouting back and forth.

Until now Lisa hadn't realized she missed her parents. Her mother was trying to tell her about all the sights they'd seen and how busy they were.

"I'll let your father talk to you now."

His voice sounded tired, and he told her he had been very busy at the Paris hospital.

"I leave most of the sightseeing to your mother, Lisa. Are you having a good time?"

She drew a deep shaky breath. "No!"

"Oh, I'm sorry, dear. But the summer will soon be gone. We miss you, darling. We love you."

Then there were hasty goodbyes to everyone, and the connection was broken. Grandma hung up with a sigh.

"Imagine, talking all the way to Paris!"

"That's a first for us," Grandpa grinned.

"I think your mother's having a fabulous time, Lisa," Grandpa said. "I'm so glad. And your father is working hard, but I'm sure he thinks the trip was worthwhile."

"Yeah," Lisa said grumpily.

She went back to her room. The phone call had made her feel worse instead of better. They were having a great time, and she was trapped here in this house on a farm in Iowa and not having a good time at all! It wasn't fair. Why hadn't they taken her along like she wanted?

When she came downstairs the next morning, Grandpa had gone outside. Her breakfast waited for her on the table. Grandma had gone down to the Shaws again.

She made a face. Were they trying to make her feel all the more guilty?

The thought made her angry. Well, she was darned if she would stay around all morning and watch the house! Whistling to Teddy, she struck off for the creek, armed with a book and some stationery to write to Brad.

The creek sparkled along, whispering against the banks. Teddy stretched beside her, thumping his tail.

"Hi!"

She looked up to find Charlie coming toward her.

"I thought I'd find you here since you weren't at the house," Charlie said.

Seeing Charlie Shaw just now wasn't exactly making her jump for joy. She was in no mood for him!

He sat down beside her, stretching out his long legs and leaning back on the palms of his hands. "Pretty day," he sighed. "Man, wouldn't it be something if every day was like this?"

"Isn't there any place around here where a person can have some privacy?" she asked coldly.

Charlie's cheeks colored. He hunched his legs up under his chin, wrapping his arms around them. Now and then he reached down to stroke Teddy's head, pensive.

"I just wanted to talk to you about something," he said. "Sorry. I didn't mean to crash in on your space, Lisa."

Then he got quickly to his feet and walked away, shoulders sagging, muttering to himself.

Lisa put her head back and closed her eyes. Oh, great! Now Charlie was mad at her, too! Angrily she snatched up a clod of dirt and tossed it into the creek, making the water spray silver in the sunlight. Teddy wiggled his ears and looked at her.

It was useless to try to read now. Her concentration was shattered. She began a letter to Brad and then crumpled it. That was useless, too!

But she stayed at the creek until it was time to go home and fix Grandpa some lunch. She had never known much about cooking but Grandpa didn't complain about what she put on the table for him.

"I hear Charlie's got a bumper crop of watermelons," he said.

She sighed. Grandpa acted as if that melon patch was a gold mine!

"He's going to supply Reynolds for the Watermelon Festival. He's sold the rest to a supermarket in Bloomhurst."

Lisa had a sudden thought.

"When is the Watermelon Festival?"

"The weekend after next."

The idea took root through the afternoon and when Grandma came home, she put the question to her straight out. "You said once that maybe I could invite Brad to come and visit."

Grandma nodded. "Yes, I did."

"Well, couldn't he come for the Watermelon Festival?"

Grandma thought about it for a moment. "Matter of fact, I think that might be the perfect time for him to visit. The festival is fun, and you could entertain him there."

"Oh, Grandma!"

She hadn't been so happy in ages. With a laugh she gave her grandmother a quick grin.

"Thanks. I'll write him right now. Oh, it will be great to see him again."

Grandma gave her a warm smile. "I guess you

have been lonely. I didn't realize that. I'm sorry. Perhaps I've forgotten what it is to be so young."

Lisa was halfway up to her room for her stationery when she turned back. "Grandma . . . I'm sorry about yesterday . . . I mean, I shouldn't have left like that."

"Water under the bridge!" Grandma said. "Oh, it's good to see you happy again, Lisa."

"You, too, Grandma."

Then with a laugh Lisa rushed up the steps, and by the time she got to her room, she was singing, her heart soaring with anticipation at the prospect of seeing Brad again.

Chapter 9 _____

The words fairly flew over the pages as Lisa wrote to Brad to extend the invitation. She knew a Watermelon Festival didn't sound like a very big thing, and she tried to paint it as brightly as she could.

The next morning, with Teddy tagging at her heels, she went to put it in the big mailbox at the end of the lane where the rural mail carrier would pick it up when he made his rounds in his rattly jeep.

"Just think, Teddy, I'll be seeing Brad again — in just a few days. I can't wait!"

Even before she knew the letter could have reached Brad, she began to wait for a reply. Two days passed, three, then four.

"Surely tomorrow," she said with a sigh as she plucked the mail from the box, seeing at once there was no letter for her.

Teddy barked softly and wagged his tail. She put her fingers into his thick fur and paused a minute to look down the road toward the Shaw house. Charlie had made himself scarce since their last encounter at the stream. She didn't know why she should let it bother her. Charlie was not that important to her. Even if she did remember that night at the lake with a pang sometimes.

Once again her old friend Jody crossed her mind. She and Charlie were alike in some ways. Honest and strong. Tuned into wavelengths Lisa sometimes didn't hear at all. She shook away the thought. In a minute she'd be rushing down the road to find Charlie and apologize to him! And *he* was the one who had come tromping into her privacy and evading it like some unthinking clod.

She carried the mail back to the kitchen, and Grandma gave her a quick smile. "Would you mind doing an errand for me? I promised Sue this roast for their supper tonight. Could you take it down for me?"

"Oh, gee, Grandma, do I have to?"

"I would appreciate it," she said.

Lisa sighed and finally nodded. "Okay. I'll do it. Then I think I'll go down to the stream."

Grandma laughed and put the foil-wrapped roast in Lisa's arms. "A good day for it. Sometime I'm going to join you — just kiss all the work goodbye and take off."

"You *never* do that!" Lisa frowned. "Nor does Grandpa. Honestly, all you two ever do is work, work, work."

"Not true," Grandma sighed. "It just seems like it to you. I suppose it is different from things at home."

Home! What a bittersweet word. Whistling to Teddy, she placed the roast in the basket on the bike and wheeled away down the lane. The collie trotted along beside her, racing happily, tongue hanging out. He found it great fun to keep pace with her, and more than once, he ran a circle around her, barking joyfully.

The Shaw place hadn't changed an iota since the first time she saw it. Charlie materialized from under The Heap and held a greasy wrench in his hand. A smear of the black goo was across the front of his shirt, and he'd skinned a knuckle.

"Hi," he said.

She managed a smile in return. "Hi."

"Still sore at me?"

"I never said I was sore at you!" she exploded. "Why does everyone around here have to blow everything out of proportion?"

He shook his fingers, letting them dangle from his bony wrist as if he had been burned. "Ouch! Sorry. Still touchy, I see. Hey, why don't I show you my melon patch? You won't believe how they've grown. Ah, those green beauties! They're going to line my pockets. And if everyone brags them up at the festival this year, I'll get the contract for the melons again!"

"Charlie, it may come as a surprise to you, but not everyone is so gung-ho about your melons!"

Charlie wasn't going to be angered this time. He started cleaning his hands. Then tossing tools into a battered tool box, he wouldn't take no for an answer. The melon patch was beyond her imagination.

"I can't believe it! They've all swelled up so. They're so *big*! When I last saw them, they were little and round like — "

"Green golf balls." Charlie grinned. "It's a combination of things, Lisa. Rain at the right time, the right soil, and good seed." The sun was warm and bright in the melon patch. A bee droned around their heads and then soared away. Far away Lisa throught she could hear the sound of Grandpa's weed mower. Suddenly Charlie flung his arms up into the air and shouted.

"Wahoo!" he whooped. "Wahoo! I did it. I got me the best old watermelon patch in the county! Man, I can't wait to start the harvest. I've got some wagons already borrowed. I'll take a load to Bloomhurst. I'll save out the choice ones for the festival."

Lisa laughed. "Charlie, you really *are* crazy!"

He sobered suddenly and gave her that direct look she had come to know. "Is Brad coming to the festival?"

"How did you know about that?"

"Marge told me you were going to invite him. Is he coming?"

"I don't know yet."

"I'm anxious to meet him. I'm real curious, Lisa."

She lifted her chin. "You won't like him."

He looked puzzled. "Why? I like you. Seems like we get along most of the time. So if you like *me*, then you must like my sort. So it stands to reason that Brad —"

She nearly laughed in his face. Comparing himself to Brad! Kevin, yes, but Charlie — never. She turned to go, saying she wanted to get back. Charlie fell in step at last, sensing her mood as he often did, saying very little.

When they reached her bike, Charlie took hold of the handlebars for a minute to detain her. "Going to the stream?" he asked.

"Yes."

"I don't suppose you want company. I could get a couple of cans of cold soda, and we could toast all the little fishes and the wild violets."

"There are no wild violets. It's past their season."

"But there are some wild roses down there and always the dandelions."

She shook her head. "Only you, Charlie Shaw, would want to toast a dandelion!" She rushed away, pedaling furiously.

That afternoon, the phone rang about one-thirty, just as Lisa was folding the tea towel. Grandma had donned her sun hat for another weeding session in the flower beds.

"Hey, Lisa!" Kevin said in his deep, rumbling voice. "Want to go for a spin?"

"Love it!" she laughed. "You've just saved me from a boring afternoon."

"Nothing's boring when we're together," he said with a purring sound in his voice. "We make sparks, you know that."

"Hmm. Keep talking, I'm listening."

"No time. Terry's breathing down my neck to hurry up. Half an hour."

"Gotcha."

Lisa hung up and rushed upstairs to change her clothes and freshen up. Pulling on a pair of white shorts and a brilliant blue top, she looked at herself in the mirror. Her cheeks were slightly flushed; her eyes were shining. She'd picked up a glorious tan. Brad would be surprised when he saw her. She looked — well — she couldn't find the word. Filled out, matured — it must be Grandma's cooking.

With the Terrible Three, Lisa whiled away an hour or so in a local place, sipping Pepsis and dancing. As she whirled about to the music, she thought of Brad, sitting on his throne at the Centerville swimming pool, her bronzed god. Oh, how she wished she could have seen him all these lazy summer days and lain there in the sun close to him, listening to his voice, seeing his eyes flash, swimming with him, doing her best to outrace him.

Brad! A tremble went over her. Why didn't he get in touch? Why didn't he write? He *had* to come. Oh, if he didn't! She wouldn't let such thoughts enter her head. Not for a moment.

They were ten minutes late getting her home. But if Grandma noticed, she didn't say anything. Lisa pitched right in with setting the table and helping Grandma finish peeling the potatoes. Grandpa had been working outside and came in from the basement, his tanned, weathered face scrubbed and shiny.

"What did you do today?" Grandma asked.

Lisa shrugged. "Oh, the usual. We had some Pepsis, danced a little, drove around, talked to some other kids, decided not to go swimming, talked about the festival. We talked about Brad."

"And you had a good time doing that?" Grandpa asked.

"I had a marvelous time!" she replied, nearly shouting.

Grandma sent Grandpa a meaningful look, and he said no more, but Lisa knew that he very plainly, loud and clear, thought the entire afternoon had been wasted. Unless she was raising pigs or tinkering with a car or cooking meals like the Shaw kids, she didn't amount to a hill of beans! How unfair could he be?

Two more days went by, and there was still no letter from Brad. Thankfully the Terrible Three came every day.

Then finally, with the festival near at hand, a letter arrived, a short note written in Brad's heavy hand.

"I'll be arriving Thursday on the afternoon bus. Roll out those melons, baby. Dying to see you." It was signed, "Brad."

She read the note with her heart thundering, then ran all the way back to the house, shouting for Grandma.

"He's coming! He's coming, Grandma. Thursday on the afternoon bus. Oh, Grandma — Brad's coming!"

Grandma gave her a happy smile. "I should bake some extra cookies, and I was wondering . . . what does he like to eat? I'll make something special for him."

"Grandma, you're super!"

The world was suddenly so bright and shiny, it nearly blinded her. She went into a frenzied activity. There was so much to do. She spent hours deciding which outfit to wear when they went to meet him, shampooed her hair on Wednesday, and brushed it more than a hundred times. She fussed about the guest room, making certain everything was just perfect for him.

The hours crawled by.

"Thursday will never come!" she wailed.

"Don't wish your life away," Grandpa said with a wink. "It will get here, all in its own time."

Grandma baked and fixed food as if she were expecting royalty. It warmed Lisa's heart. Mother had never done that for Brad. Her parents didn't even like him! Grandma was prepared to think he was special, just on Lisa's say-so.

She slept fitfully Wednesday night. Thursday morning she decided to shampoo her hair again. She changed her mind twice about her outfit and finally went back to her original plans.

At last Thursday afternoon came, and they were on their way into town. Lisa couldn't remember a time she'd been so nervous, unless it was the day Brad came up to the plate during the last game of the baseball tournament. She'd never forget the sound of his bat sending that ball over the fence for a homer.

She thought she would die waiting for the bus. The town was so quiet, so tiny. She'd become used to it now, but suddenly she knew how it would look through Brad's appraising eyes. Her nervousness grew. Maybe it hadn't been such a good idea, inviting him here.

Then she shook that thought away. She wanted to see him. She *needed* to see him. Somehow, living here, she wasn't the same person. She sensed something slipping away, something precious and personal, something she must not lose. Brad would put her on the right track. One look, one word, one smile, and she would be on his wavelength, and together they could do anything.

"It's coming," Grandpa said calmly.

Lisa was frozen. As if in a dream, she climbed out of the car and stood waiting for the bus to lurch to a halt with a hiss of its air brakes.

She saw his long legs, his bronzed arms, the jazzy duffel bag he carried, and then there he was. At last. Her wonderful, handsome, tremendous Brad!

"Hey!" he said when he caught sight of her.

Then with a grin he swept her up into his arms and, right in front of Grandma and Grandpa, he kissed her. The world was suddenly very beautiful and lovely again!

Chapter 10 _____

Grandpa was grinning, and Grandma came toward them, hand outstretched, a welcoming smile on her face.

"Hello, Brad! It's nice to meet you at last. I'm Marge, and this is Tom. Lisa's grandparents."

Brad nodded his head in his quick way and shook Grandpa's hand.

"I thought you'd never get here," Lisa said.

"Crummy bus was late," he replied. "Is this the only transportation into this Podunk — I mean this place?"

Grandpa shot him a quick look, but Grandma graciously overlooked the remark. True, Reynolds was barely more than a wide spot in the road, but they were used to the place. Even Lisa was used to it now.

"I see they're getting things ready for the festival," Marge said as they walked to the car. "It's quite an occasion for Reynolds."

Brad tightened his arm around Lisa's waist, but didn't say anything. She couldn't believe he was here, actually walking beside her in the hot sunlight,

106

looking down at her with wry amusement in his eyes.

The drive home was filled with talk of friends at home and his work at the swimming pool. Lisa couldn't keep her eyes off him. He was bronzed a gorgeous golden tan, and his blond hair was bleached almost white. No one wore jeans and a sport shirt with such flair.

When they passed the Shaw place, Grandpa slowed down to miss one of the wandering chickens. Brad's brow arched up.

"Good grief, what is that place?" Brad asked.

"Just the Shaws," Grandpa laughed. "It's not really as bad as it looks."

"They're happy-go-lucky," Grandma sighed. "Sometimes I think they've got a lease on life that I almost envy."

Brad was fascinated with the clutter, and as they drove on past, he craned his neck for a second look.

"So that's the Shaw place you wrote me about," he said. "I never thought it would look like that!"

Lisa was relieved when they had driven on by, and Grandpa was proudly pointing out his corn crop.

"One of the best I ever had," he said. "Just holding my breath that something doesn't happen. Fact is, the weather's been sort of muggy for several days. Probably a storm brewing."

"Don't talk about it!" Grandma scolded. "Don't even *think* it."

"I'd sure hate to see anything go wrong after bringing it along this far," Grandpa said with a worried air.

Finally they had reached the lane. Lisa was con-

107

scious of holding her breath. Sometimes Brad liked things she didn't expect him to like. But she was pretty certain the farm and the house wouldn't really impress or interest him. When they came to a stop, Brad climbed out, and Lisa followed. He looked around with critical eyes. But Grandma was hurrying them inside.

"I've got a pitcher of lemonade in the refrigerator," Grandma said. "It's so hot today, it will taste good."

Brad looked around, saying nothing. Lisa took him upstairs to show him his room, and he dumped his duffel bag on the bed.

"Hey, come here," he said in a hoarse whisper. "I couldn't really kiss you at the bus station with them looking on."

She nestled into his arms, and he kissed her for a long time.

"Oh, Brad, I've missed you!"

"Well, I'm here now."

"I thought you might have found a new girl while I was away," she teased. "I bet you had girls drooling all over you at the pool."

"Hundreds," he said quickly.

"Hundreds I can handle, it's the special one or two that worry me."

He was frowning and pushing away from her, jerking at the strings of his duffel bag. "Don't be silly," he said.

He seemed angry and on edge. She felt a whisper of uneasiness across her heart, like a cold icy wind that cut to the bone. Had he been too quick with his retort?

Grandma was calling for them to come to the kitchen.

"Good grief," Brad scowled. "Does she mother-hen you all the time like this?"

She started to answer and changed her mind. She couldn't belittle Grandma, not even for Brad.

"Come along, be a sport." She coaxed him into a better mood, and they went down to the kitchen. The lemonade was good, and he asked for a second glass, which pleased Grandma. Lisa kept pinching herself, telling herself over and over again — he's here, he's here!

Then the Terrible Three put in an appearance. Grandpa heard them coming before Lisa. With a slight frown he drew a deep breath, expelled his breath from puffed-out cheeks.

"Well, here they come, burning rubber and raising dust."

Kevin's car came to a noisy halt, and the horn began to blare. Lisa laughed at Brad's perplexed look.

"The Terrible Three. My new friends. Come on, let's go out, and you can meet them, Brad."

He was reluctant until he caught a glimpse of Kevin's jazzy car, and then he straightened with surprise. "Wow, look at those wheels."

"Come on," Lisa laughed with excitement. "Is it okay, Grandma?"

"Of course," she said with a wave of her hand. "I couldn't stop you if I tried."

After half an hour with the Terrible Three, Brad had relaxed. They were all instant friends. Kevin and Brad hit it off especially well, talking sports and automobiles. Brad tightened his arm around Lisa's shoulder, and she felt snug and secure. It was fun to be buzzing around in Kevin's car with Brad beside her. It was almost like being at home with her old friends.

At Bloomhurst they decided they'd have a pizza for supper.

"Oh, but Grandma's expecting us, Brad, we've got to get back."

He scowled at her. "Don't be a drag, Lisa. Good heavens, you never were. What's gotten into you?"

She gave him a limp smile. She knew how Grandma had planned the first meal Brad would eat with them.

"I'll have to phone."

Brad gave an exasperated smile. "Okay. Okay! They're worse than your parents, Lisa."

Somehow she managed the phone call, knowing how disappointed Grandma was. She hung up without saying goodbye, and she hated feeling so guilty and unhappy.

"You're all going to the festival, I take it," Brad was saying as Lisa joined them in a crowded booth.

Kevin wrinkled his nose. "Sure. But it doesn't take long to do that. And it's Dullsville, Brad. We usually take off and go somewhere else."

"Yeah, how much watermelon can you eat anyway?" Terry wondered.

"Well, it *is* quaint," Dina piped up. "All those corny window displays and the food counters and of course the watermelons. I hear Crazy Charlie is providing them this year."

"Crazy Charlie!" Kevin snorted. "Just about his speed."

"Hey, we were going to visit his watermelon patch, remember?" Terry said, eyes flashing. "Why not tonight? Watermelon for dessert. How about it? Is everyone game?"

"Watermelon patch?" Brad asked. "You mean you're going to raid the patch — hey — can we do that? I mean can we get away with it?"

Kevin gave them a broad wink. "Just watch and see!"

Brad grinned. "I've never done that before."

"Oh, there's a few advantages to living out here in the sticks," Kevin laughed, poking Brad in the ribs.

They began planning it carefully, deciding they must wait until it was fully dark.

Dina nudged Lisa. "Hey, you're not saying anything. Don't tell me you're not game!"

Lisa swallowed hard and put a quick smile on her face. "I'm just listening. Honestly, you fellas are planning this as if it were a bank bust or something!"

"Part of the fun," Terry grinned.

Lisa listened as they talked on and on about it, joking, and building it up and up until everyone was high on it. Everyone but her. She felt sick inside. They thought it was a harmless prank, but she knew how Charlie had nurtured every one of those green melons and how he counted on the money each one would bring.

They left the pizza parlor, drove around to show Brad what few sights there were, downed cold drinks at a drive-in, and drag-raced with another car down the main street of Bloomhurst, flirting with real trouble when the city police suddenly appeared. It was getting late.

Lisa, for one, was relieved to leave Bloomhurst behind. But she clenched her fists tightly, palms moist, and tried to laugh when the rest of them talked about raiding Charlie's melon patch. She told herself that a melon or two wouldn't even be missed. It wasn't that. It was the idea of the thing — those melons were precious to Charlie. Like Grandpa and his corn — he had worked so hard, planned and dreamed and worried about his crop. Now . . .

"Here we are," Kevin said, as he parked the car and turned the headlights off. "We'll sit here a few minutes, make sure everything is nice and quiet."

Dina snickered nervously. Terry muttered under his breath and jiggled his foot up and down. Brad was as cool as Kevin, who thought this entire caper was a blast. Lisa's cheeks burned with anguish. She gnawed at her lower lip with her teeth. Beside her, Brad was eager to get the show on the road.

"What are we going to do after you get the melons?" Lisa asked.

"Have a melon bust — maybe at your grandfather's place."

"No," Lisa said quickly. "We'd better not."

"Uptown then. In the park."

"The county sheriff patrols Reynolds," Dina said.

"Chicken!" Kevin scoffed. "How's he to know where they came from?"

"It *is* stealing," Lisa said in a small voice.

By now Terry had climbed out of the car and was slipping away in the darkness, looking around.

"Naw, it's not stealing," Kevin retorted. "It's just having a little fun at Crazy Charlie's expense."

"He must be some kind of creep for you to want to pick on him like this," Brad said.

"Why don't you like him?" Lisa asked. "You know, I really never did know why you dislike him so much, Kevin."

Kevin snorted in the darkness. "You've got to be kidding! What's to like about Charlie?"

She shrugged. "Just because he's different?"

Kevin had heard Terry's faint whistle which meant all was clear. Kevin never answered but flung open the door and motioned for them to follow him.

"Okay, gang. Let's go!"

Lisa was tugged along with them, Brad's hand hot around hers. She stumbled in the dark, not because she couldn't see, but because she had this horrible sinking sensation in the pit of her stomach that she should stay in the car. But there was no hanging back. With hoarse shrieks they were hoisting her over the fence, then running through the melon patch. The boys were arguing over which ones to take.

"Holy mackerel!" Kevin paused. "Look over there."

In the dim light of the stars Lisa saw two farm wagons heaped with melons. She knew they were either for the festival or for the supermarket at Bloomhurst.

"Charlie's already picked them for us," Kevin crowed. "Come on. Everybody grab one."

Lisa hung back. They argued over which to take, not caring that their voices were carrying on the summer breeze. Lisa's stomach lurched. But Brad was in the thick of it, having the time of his life, laughing and hugging a melon in his arms.

"Man, this thing must weight twenty-five pounds!"

"Hey," Kevin said. "Wait a minute."

Everyone hushed, and in a moment Kevin was snickering in glee.

"Put your melons over here," he said. "We'll get them later. Terry, there's a ravine over there. A deep ditch. If we all get hold of the wagon tongue and heave-ho, we could push the wagon over there and —"

Terry slapped him on the back. "Hey! Sure thing. We'll dump 'em all. I'd love to see Crazy Charlie's face in the morning when he finds his melons in a heap at the bottom of the ravine!"

"Wait a minute," Lisa said. "You'll break them!"

She was overruled, scoffed at, accused of being soft on Crazy Charlie. Even Brad fell in with Kevin's plans, and the first thing she knew, they were attacking the wagon.

"It's too damn heavy, Kevin," Brad said, puffing and panting as he put his shoulder to the wheel. "We'll never move it."

"We'll move it!" he insisted. "We've got enough manpower. Just a few feet and the field begins to slope. It will pick up speed as it goes."

Incredibly, they moved the wagon. Lisa only pretended to help. She hated all of it. The wagon moved slowly, the wheels cutting into the sandy soil, but at last they reached a point where it began to roll easier.

"Open the tailgate," Terry shouted. "They'll come out of there like torpedoes."

It took only a nudge, and the melons began to cascade out of the wagon, with some of them rolling a short distance before they made a squashing, bursting sound, while others smashed open at their feet.

Gleefully, caught up in a kind of frenzy, Terry leaped up into the wagon and began to kick at them, sending them rolling and tumbling, spilling into the dark, faster and faster. The sweet smell of the pink meat of the melons was thick in the air.

"That's all here," Kevin said. "There's another wagon over there."

"Oh, no!" Brad groaned. "We'll never get it pushed this far."

"Then we'll pitch them one at a time. Come on — hurry up — before Charlie hears us."

Lisa wouldn't participate. Even Dina hung back, pleading fatigue. But the boys made short work of the wagonload of melons, and the sound of them splattering and thudding into the silent darkness echoed inside Lisa's heart like some dreadful tolling of a bell.

Kevin leaped down from the wagon. "That ought to fix old Charlie Shaw."

"But why did you want to?" Lisa asked, a knot in her throat. "Why?"

Terry laughed and slapped Kevin on the back. "Oh, it's an old grudge. Truth is, Charlie and Kevin met in the wrestling ring at school last year. Charlie pinned Kevin so fast, it would make your head spin.

He never lived it down, did you, Kevin? Crazy Charlie making a fool out of you like that."

"Shut up!" Kevin barked. "Just shut up, Terry. You always talk too darned much. Let's get out of here."

They were all in a rush now. The fun was over. It was time to leave. Lugging three of the melons, the boys rushed to the car, the girls following.

Once there, Kevin put the car in gear and, as his last vicious act, deliberately roared by the Shaw house.

They ate the melons by a street light, broken as they were by being dropped on a picnic table. Everyone snatched pieces of the sweet pink flesh of the melon's heart, savoring its sweetness. Lisa pretended to find it tasty, a stiff smile on her face, an awkward laugh on her lips. But the sweetness was bitter on her tongue. Her throat could scarcely swallow it. She ate very little.

They washed their hands and faces at an outside faucet, and then, because it was very late, Lisa said they must get home. Brad made no protest. It seemed a long way to the house. She felt heavy of heart, sick to her stomach, empty, and a little soiled.

"We'll come out tomorrow," Kevin said. "Find something to do."

"Great," Brad called back. "Better than spending a day in this place. I never was a hayseed."

They laughed at that as if it was the greatest joke in the world. Lisa was glad when they had driven away.

"Grandpa and Grandma have gone to bed," she said tiredly. "I think we'd better go, too, Brad."

He muttered something under his breath, but finally agreed. "Okay. Okay. Don't get upset. You're sure uptight, Lisa. Your summer here must have been something else!"

"Yeah," she murmured. "It has been."

She couldn't say goodnight quickly enough or escape into her room fast enough.

The fresh country air stirred the curtains at the window. She almost imagined she could smell the broken melons in the ravine, their sweet fragrance wafting on the night air.

How could she have let them do it? Why had they thought it was such great fun? And Brad had been right in it, along with Kevin, laughing and having a ball.

She closed her eyes. She would not think about it. Maybe it wasn't really as bad as she'd imagined. Charlie had a jillion melons. Besides, it was an old country custom to raid watermelon patches. Kevin had said so.

But all the same, she didn't think she could eat a piece of watermelon and enjoy it ever again.

Chapter 11 _____

The breeze at the window suddenly died. The
heat was oppressive in the room. Lisa had never
heard such a frightening stillness. Curious, she got
up to peer outside into the darkness. The stars were
gone. It was black as pitch out there!

Almost instantly, the moment she realized something was wrong, Grandma was rapping at the door.
A cold chill raced over Lisa.

"Go to the basement! Hurry!" Grandma said.
"Hurry! I think there's a tornado."

With a screech of fear Lisa grabbed a robe and
slippers and collided with a very sleepy Brad in the
hallway.

Grandpa was rushing them down to the basement, his flashlight showing them the way.

Lisa remembered the first time she had come
here to wait out a storm and how odd and bizarre it
had seemed. She had wanted Brad to experience it
so they could laugh about it. This time it was no
laughing matter.

"Oh, great jumping cats!" Grandpa said. "Listen
to that!"

118

It began as a strange whining sound, and soon it was roaring like a freight train headed straight for the basement. Grandma snatched at Lisa.

"Under the table. Quick!"

Grandpa was urging Brad to follow suit, and incredibly all of them were wedged under an old dining room table that Grandma used for a work area.

The wind was howling and roaring. The house seemed to tremble and shake. Terrible noises were mixing in with the roar. Something crashed against the house. Glass shattered. Grandma was holding Lisa close, but her arms were trembling, and as she pressed her cheek to Lisa's, Lisa felt the hot salty tears streaming down her grandmother's face. She clung to her all the more and realized for the first time that her grandmother was every bit as frightened as she was.

It seemed to last an eternity. The roar was deafening, and then abruptly it seemed to be gone. Rain and hail pelted the house, and as they all waited, spellbound, they realized the tornado had passed over them.

"The house must still be intact," Grandpa breathed. "Thank God!"

"Oh, Tom, Tom," Grandma said.

Grandpa gave her a hug and helped them out from under the table. "We'll stay here a while. Just to be sure the worst is over."

Nervously the four of them perched on old chairs or boxes. Grandpa turned out the flashlight to save the battery, and through the small basement windows the lightning brightened the room.

"Does this happen often?" Brad asked.

"We haven't had a really bad tornado in the neighborhood for twenty years. But the weather is more severe than it used to be. Bloomhurst is hit nearly ever summer, it seems. Mostly taking a building or two and lots of trees," Grandpa replied.

"Shouldn't we go and look to see if there's damage?" Brad asked.

"Not just yet," Grandpa said. "Sometimes these things turn around and come back, and when they do, you'd better find a hole to hide in!"

Fresh fear churned inside Lisa's stomach. But the rain seemed to be slackening off now, and the lightning had ceased to flash so severely. The thunder began to rumble farther and farther away.

Grandpa took a quick tour of the house and came back to report that except for one broken window upstairs, nothing seemed to be damaged inside.

"Outside is probably another matter. Too dark now. It will have to wait until morning. I think it's safe to go back to bed."

After all the excitement Lisa didn't think she would sleep, but she did. When she awakened the next morning, the skies were clear. The air at the window smelled fresh and clean, rain-washed. She stared out. The old apple tree in the backyard was down, its trunk twisted and wrenched to the ground by the vicious wind. Shingles were off the barn. Her stomach sank to her shoes when she saw the rows of corn flattened against the ground.

"Oh, no!"

Dressing quickly, she tore down the steps. Grandpa was on the back porch, taking off a pair of muddy overshoes. His overalls were wet up to the knees, and the look in his eyes brought a new sickness to Lisa.

"The corn's ruined," he said in an empty voice. "I may salvage one field. It looks as if some huge roller came over it and crushed it."

Lisa swallowed hard. She'd never seen such a look of defeat in her Grandpa's eyes.

"But it will straighten up, Grandpa!" she said. "It did before."

He shook his head and took a long time in retying a shoelace. "Not this time, hon. This time the stalks are broken off at the ground. Like someone took a scythe to them and cut them right off."

His voice broke. His shoulders sagged as if the weight of the world had just been dropped on them.

"Oh, Grandpa!" Lisa said with sorrow in her voice. "All that hard work, all that expense."

He lifted his head for a moment and gave her a tired smile. "That's the way it goes sometimes when you're a farmer."

"What will you do?"

"What we've done more than once before. Manage somehow on a short crop. Borrow money next spring so we can plant again."

He put out a long arm and pulled her close for a moment. She put a kiss on the top of his white hair.

"I'm so sorry, Grandpa."

"Guess you are at that," he said. "Nice to know. Well, we mustn't let Marge see us like this. It's not going to make her a bit happy."

She watched him stand up and gather his strength

and courage around him until he seemed taller than ever, and when he walked inside to where Marge was busy fixing breakfast, he was able to give her a confident nod of his head.

"We're hurt bad, Marge. Probably only got thirty or forty acres of corn still standing. But we'll make out, darlin', we always do."

Marge went pale and clutched at her apron with shaking hands. "Oh, Tom."

It was a solemn breakfast. Brad asked a million questions, and patiently Grandpa gave him all the answers he could. As they were having a second helping of scrambled eggs, Lisa heard The Heap come rattling down the lane.

"Here's Charlie," Grandpa said. "I hope they weren't hit."

"Wouldn't take much to blow down that place," Brad scoffed.

Then Charlie was standing in the doorway, a tall, rangy boy with a vacant look in his eyes.

"Did you have any damage?" Grandpa asked.

"No. Lucked out. I see it got your corn, Tom," Charlie said.

"Yes," Grandpa nodded. "Is everyone okay at your house?"

Charlie gave him a wry grin. "Everybody but me. It's my melons —"

Beneath the table Brad gave Lisa a sudden kick and flashed her a silly grin. Lisa wanted the floor to open up and swallow her.

"The wind?" Grandpa asked. "You mean the wind did something to the melons?"

"Like to think it was that," Charlie said. "Seems

as if two wagonloads were dumped into the ravine last night."

"What!" Grandma asked. "You mean the wind picked up the wagons and —"

"Naw," Charlie shook his head. "Not the wind. Of course, the rain washed out the tracks, but I figure it was some two-legged animals that did it. Opened up the tailgate and let the melons roll down. Smashed ninety percent of them."

"Of all the low-down, dirty tricks!" Grandpa exploded. "You had those melons loaded for the supermarket at Bloomhurst!"

"Just one load was for them. The other was for the festival. I'll drive over and tell them I can't deliver."

"What about the festival?" Lisa managed to ask.

"Probably run short, but I'll scrounge around and get what I can. Maybe have to go somewhere and buy from someone over around the river. Course, they'll charge me more than I've got them sold for. Looks like I'll be in the hole."

Grandma was dumbfounded. Filled with sympathy, she did what she could to cheer him up, offering him breakfast or a loan of money if he needed it.

"I'm okay," Charlie said. "Just darned lucky we didn't lose the house and everything else. Darned lucky."

Then he said goodbye and went away. Grandpa stood in the doorway watching him go. "Now why would anyone want to do that to a boy like Charlie?" he wondered.

Lisa couldn't eat another bite. She asked to be

excused from the table. Grandma, still thinking about Charlie's news, didn't realize Lisa was blinking back tears.

Once upstairs she vomited in the bathroom and bathed her face in cool water. It was all she could do that day to look anyone in the eye. She was grateful that later Grandpa enlisted their help in clearing away the old apple tree and some of the other trash caused by trees blown down around the farm.

Brad wanted to show how strong he was and tried to impress Grandpa. But Grandpa could work circles around him and scarcely noticed his athletic prowess. His thoughts were clearly on the destroyed cornfields. Lisa's heart ached for him. She felt so miserable, she wished she could run away and hide. Even Teddy, who often sensed her moods, couldn't cheer her, even when he pushed his nose into her hand and rubbed his soft fur against her.

The festival was still planned. Everyone had this feverish idea that the celebration must go on, no matter what.

"They're crazy," Brad scoffed. "What's so important about a corny festival?"

"It's an annual affair. Sort of a neighborly get-together," Lisa said. "Everyone works hard to see that it goes off with a bang."

"Yeah, I guess so," Brad said. "If you're not careful, Lisa, you're going to be as much of a hick as some of the others around here."

She struggled to say something but decided it was best just to keep still. Brad gave her a quick kiss. "It won't be long until you'll be home in Centerville where you belong. Then you'll get your head on straight again."

The day of the festival the sun was bright and the skies so blue and deep that no one would have dreamed that just days ago the tornado had ripped its way through the countryside.

The Terrible Three were going to pick up Brad and Lisa. Grandma and Grandpa promised to see them at the festival.

At last they were off. Kevin buzzed the car along the road, but slowed down near town when he hit traffic. Who would have thought so many people would turn out for such an event?

The main street was roped off, and various stands lined the sidewalks. There were refreshments, a few craft displays, and at the far end, several long tables filled with watermelons cut into generous slices. Everyone was invited to eat his fill free of charge. Behind one table, Charlie was being assisted by Sue and Lennie.

"Hey, let's go get some melon," Kevin whispered.

"Yeah," Terry agreed. "Come on, gang!"

Lisa hung back. But the rest of them went up boldly to the table and took their sweet time in selecting the slice of melon they wanted.

"Seems kind of skimpy," Kevin said, eyeing the nearly empty wagons behind Charlie. "You're going to run short."

"I heard you had a bumper crop. What happened to it?" Terry piped up.

Charlie was keeping his cool, but the way his gaze swept over the three boys, Lisa was certain he suspected them of being the vandals in his melon patch.

"Had some really hard luck, I hear," Terry said, unwilling to let it lie. "I heard someone smashed up some of your melons. That's a real shame. Any idea who did it?"

Charlie reached behind him for another melon, and with his long, supple hands and a very sharp knife he sliced the melon, the cracking sound revealing the pink meat inside. But still he said nothing.

"Well, come on, folks," Kevin said airily. "Better amble on. Charlie's got to cut up some more melons. Sure hope you don't run out."

Then with a cocky swagger Kevin led the way, and the rest of them followed. Only Lisa lingered behind.

"Charlie —"

"Better run along or you'll get left," Charlie told her.

"I'm really sorry about your melons," she said.

He gave her a direct look, searched her eyes and her face, and she felt the warmth come to her cheeks.

"It's okay, Lisa. I'll manage."

He gave her his friendly grin, and she saw the way he straightened and squared his shoulders. His disappointment and bitterness must have been deep, but he wasn't letting it show. He was like Grandpa, gritting his teeth and going on, thinking about next year's harvest, determined it would be better. Strange, this strength possessed by people who worked the soil, who planted the seeds and watched the weather and prayed for rain. How special they were!

"Nothing to do here," Kevin was complaining. "Unless you want to ride that ratty old Ferris wheel."

"Not in a million years," Brad scoffed. "It looks like it's seen better days. I thought you promised some fun, Kevin."

"Gotcha!" Kevin laughed. "Let's get the show on the road."

It was a long, exhausting day. They crammed it with fun and laughter, doing every crazy thing they could think of. Every now and then Kevin would burst out in a guffaw.

"That hayseed! I don't think he even guessed it was us that busted his melons!" Kevin hooted. "How can you be so dumb?"

The day ended at last at about nine o'clock, when Kevin finally drove them to the farm house.

"Probably won't see you tomorrow," Kevin said. "Got this family thing I have to do."

"I'll be leaving tomorrow afternoon anyway," Brad said. "I have to report to work at the pool on Monday. Nice meeting you people. See you around."

Tomorrow, Brad would be gone. Strange, Lisa wasn't certain just how she felt about that.

The next day before leaving for the station, Lisa and Brad walked down to the stream.

"I spend a lot of time here," Lisa said, looking at the tiny stream, still swelled with the recent rain. "I write all my letters to you down here. Why don't you answer me more often, Brad?"

He lifted his shoulders in a shrug. "I told you — busy."

"Not that busy."

"Ah, heck, Lisa, you know I hate to write letters."

"What do you do with all your time off?"

"Mess around — like always. Why the third degree?" he asked a bit crossly.

She fought off the idea that had plagued her several times since he'd been here. "Are you seeing someone else?" she asked pointedly.

He heaved a big sigh and looked at her angrily. "Look, I see lots of kids. We hang out at the old places. What am I supposed to do, lock myself up in a room and pine for you?"

She was angry. "There *is* someone else!"

"Oh, shut up, Lisa. Just shut up, will you?"

He was grinning at her, erasing all her doubts as he reached for her. "Kiss me goodbye here, will you? I hate to do it in front of your nosey grandparents."

Walking back to the house, she was wishing she could hold back time. "I hate for you to go," she said.

"You'll be okay. The Terrible Three are great kids. I'm glad you've got some friends to see you through. Anyway, how much longer have you got — three weeks?"

"Something like that."

"I'll be waiting for you when you get home."

Grandpa had the car out of the garage and had placed Brad's duffel bag in the back seat. Grandma came out of the house, calling to them that it was time to go.

The drive to town only took a few minutes. They parked in the shade until, half an hour past schedule, the bus came rolling in. Brad leaped out. He politely said goodbye to Lisa's grandparents and thanked them for their hospitality. Brad had such good manners. It made Lisa's heart swell.

He squeezed her hand, and then with a wave he hoisted his duffel bag to his broad shoulder and climbed up the steps. He was the only passenger to board. In a wink of an eye he was gone.

Grandpa started the motor. Craning her neck, Lisa watched until the bus turned the corner and was gone. She leaned back, not realizing how deeply she sighed.

Chapter 12 _____

Lisa experienced a terrible letdown. Brad was gone. All summer long she had dreamed about his being here. Even for just a few days! Now the dream was over; it was a past event. It had not lived up to her expectations, and she knew it had been marred by the incident of Charlie's melon patch.

Lisa was restless and on edge. But it wasn't just that she was lonely or that she missed Brad. It was something more. Something had changed for her. She couldn't think of Charlie without wincing inwardly.

The next day, Kevin phoned. He asked her to go for an all-day outing with the Terrible Three. But she found herself making an excuse not to join them.

"Hey, what is this? With Brad gone, it must be mighty lonesome out there. Come on, be a sport."

"Not today, Kevin. Maybe next time."

She was stunned that she had actually turned them down. A week ago, she would have jumped at the chance. Now, everything was changed. She didn't want to be with them and wasn't even certain she liked them. She wished it was time to go back to Centerville. Three long weeks. Twenty-one days.

She had had numerous cards and letters from her parents. Dad's notes were always hurried and brief; he was working very hard. Mother's letters were longer and breezy. She was obviously having a good time, but she ended every letter with how much she missed Lisa. Lisa wondered if that were really true. She and Mother had not been close in the last couple of years, not really since Brad had come into the picture.

"You've changed," Mother used to say when they had one of their many arguments. "You don't talk like Lisa, you talk like Brad!"

"That's silly!" she had retorted. "Completely silly!"

"He has too much influence over you. I don't like it, Lisa. You must be your own person, not a carbon copy of someone else."

She hadn't thought about that conversation in a long time.

Lisa tried to fill her days the best she could. She read a great deal, walked with Teddy, helped Grandma in the flower beds, and in general, moped around the house like a lost puppy.

Grandma saw how she felt and did her best to cheer her up.

"You miss Brad, don't you?"

"Yes," she said.

"You know," Grandma said, loosening the dirt around one of her precious flowers, "you've got a birthday coming up in a few days."

She looked up with a start. "I'd forgotten!"

"My, my, I thought only us 'old folks' did that," Grandma teased.

Lisa flushed. "Brad must have forgotten it, too. He never even mentioned it!"

"Well, your grandfather and I haven't forgotten it. And neither have your parents. A large box arrived a couple of days ago from Paris with instructions not to give it to you until your birthday."

"A package from Paris?" she asked excitedly. "Oh, Grandma, I've got to see it! Where is it?"

"In due time." She shook her head, tossing the trowel aside.

"Grandma . . ."

"Hmm?" she asked.

"What are you hatching in that head of yours?"

Grandma laughed. "A party. A big birthday party for you. Would you like that?"

"But Grandma — you don't have to —"

"You can invite who you please. The Shaws will come, of course, and if you want to ask your new friends . . ."

With a flush of warmth coming to her cheeks, Lisa remembered another time Grandma had invited them, the day they finished walking the beans, but they hadn't seen fit to stay.

"I'll bake the cake myself," Grandma said. "I'm pretty good at decorating. We'll have a lawn party, Japanese lanterns and things like that. Won't that be fun?"

For days all the talk was about the party, and it was hard not to catch some of Grandma's enthusiasm. Even Grandpa seemed interested, and for the first time since the tornado and the loss of his corn crop, he smiled and laughed heartily.

Jonas joined Lisa at the stream a few times before the party. He came quietly, giving her a shy grin, not certain if he should intrude.

"It's okay," she told him, most of the time. "In fact, I brought a book to read. One of my mother's old ones that she left here at the house."

"Let's see!" Jonas said. It was an excuse to wiggle close, to snuggle against her. She delighted in the way his eyes sparkled with excitement as she read aloud to him. Later they would romp together in the green grass or splash water on each other from the creek. Teddy, not to be outdone, would bark and run around them, itching to be in the thick of things.

Some far corner of her heart knew that these were some of the best of times to be had. She knew that later, in some distant tomorrow, perhaps when she had children of her own, she would remember these bittersweet times with little Jonas.

One evening, as she sat on the step, watching the sun sink lower in the sky, she heard a car coming. It could only be Kevin. Sliding to a halt, stirring gravel and dust, she saw her old friends inside. Kevin climbed out to come and speak to her.

"Hey, where have you been hiding? And why haven't you called?" he demanded.

"No reason. Just . . . busy."

"You're not busy now," he said. "Come on. We're going to Bloomhurst. We'll probably go to the drive-in movie." She hesitated, knowing full well that she didn't want to go with them. She refused politely, but Kevin wasn't to be put off that easily.

"What's got into you?"

She flushed. "I haven't much time left here and there are special family things planned."

He glowered at her angrily. "It's more than that. What's happened?"

She lifted her chin but didn't answer, giving him a long, steady look.

"It's Charlie and the melons, isn't it?"

She straightened. "It was a rotten thing to do, Kevin, and all of you know it!"

"And that matters?" he asked incredulously. "You're uptight because of Crazy Charlie?"

"I hate what we did."

He shook his head slowly, still disbelieving. Then he strode back to the car and jerked open the door.

"Okay, if that's the way you want it, you've got it!"

With a roar of the engine and a spin of the wheels, Kevin shot his car out of the drive. With a kind of tired sigh, one of relief one moment and regret the next, Lisa knew she had seen the last of them.

"Lisa —" Grandma called from the kitchen door.

"Yes, Grandma."

"Did you invite them to your birthday party?"

"No," she said stiffly. "They won't be here."

"I don't understand —"

"Never mind," Lisa said tiredly. "Just don't ask questions, okay?"

Her birthday finally arrived, and the weather was perfect. Lisa had grown used to the clear blue skies and loved the fleecy clouds. At home in Centerville, she didn't often pay attention to the sky. Here it

134

was part of the landscape, a part of life. Grandpa checked it every morning for the signs of coming weather.

"I'm a weather prophet," he used to boast. "Going to rain before morning."

When it didn't, she and Grandma teased him about it by the hour.

The lawn was festive, there was no other word for it. The Japanese lanterns swung in the breeze, the lawn had been mowed to perfection, and Grandma's flowers were blooming furiously, putting on their best faces for her.

Lisa was nervous. There were no two ways about it. How could she face Charlie, talk with him, laugh, be happy, act like a birthday girl — when all the time she felt so horribly guilty and ashamed?

"Here they come," Grandma called.

The Heap was rattling its way down the lane, and all of the Shaws had crowded inside. Charlie unwound himself from behind the wheel and barely glanced at her, hurrying away into the garage, carrying a big cardboard box with him.

"You can have it later, after the cake and ice cream," he told her.

He seemed friendly. His smile was as crooked and sincere as ever. But there was something in his eyes that was different. There were no longer such direct looks shot in her direction. His gaze was veiled by his long, dark lashes.

It was impossible not to enter into the fun of things.

By the time they got down to the food, dusk had fallen, and the sky was a raspberry stain in the west, smudging the roof of the barn, the edges of the house, the trees, and the garage where the mysterious box waited.

Charlie sat opposite her, and once he reached out across the table to touch her hand. "Listen, did you hear that?" he asked.

"A dove?"

"Love to hear them."

"It's a lonely sound."

"Sometimes," he said. "Depends on who you're with, doesn't it?"

After the food was eaten, the gifts were presented to Lisa, and she opened them with care. Jonas was hanging over her shoulder, as eager as she to see what was inside.

Fran must have picked out all of the Shaws' gifts — bottles of cologne and pretty boxes of stationery. Jonas was especially proud of the silver pen he gave her with her name engraved on it.

Grandma had made her a lovely blouse, matching the exact blue of her eyes, and Grandpa, being the practical one, slipped her a twenty-dollar bill.

"Buy something foolish," he said with a wink. "You're only young once."

She was conscious of waiting for Charlie's gift as she opened the box from Paris and exclaimed over the lovely sweater and skirt her parents had sent. At last Charlie went to retrieve the box from the garage.

"Open it," Charlie said. "He's getting awfully lonesome in there."

The lid had large air holes punched in it, and something alive was wiggling inside!

"A puppy!" she gasped. "A collie puppy!"

The little ball of brown-and-white fur had bright eyes and a wagging tail. She adored him the moment she saw him. Picking him up, she began to coo to him and cuddle him, pressing her cheek against his soft fur.

"Oh, Charlie, he's beautiful!"

Charlie grinned happily. "He's marked a little like Teddy. That's why I picked him out of the litter."

Lisa felt squeamish inside. Such a wonderful gift after what she had helped do to him! How could she accept it? Then she remembered something Grandpa had said. A dog didn't belong in a city on a busy street. "It's a crime to put them on a leash or keep them locked up in a shed. A dog is supposed to run free — like Teddy."

She swallowed hard. "Oh, Charlie. I'm not sure I can keep him."

The joy went out of his eyes. He stiffened. "But why not?"

She explained, and Grandpa had to nod in agreement. "Afraid she's right."

"Lots of people have pets in town," Sue argued.

Even Lennie jumped to her defense. "That's right, Tom. Besides, Lisa would take good care of him and see that he didn't get run over or anything."

"You're outnumbered, Tom," Grandma said.

"Seems I am," he grinned. "Well, keep him while you're here anyway, Lisa. Decide later."

Charlie relaxed a little. When Lisa put the puppy down, he went waddling around the lawn. When Teddy saw him, he sniffed him curiously and decided to accept him. The rest of the evening Teddy stayed close to the puppy as if to protect him.

Lisa suddenly found herself alone with Charlie.

"I haven't been seeing much of you," he said.

"You know how it is," she said quickly. "It's always busy around here."

"It's more than that," Charlie said. "It's Brad all the way, isn't it?"

She lifted her chin. He was giving her an easy way out. "Yes, I think it is, Charlie."

She saw a slight droop come to his shoulders even though a slight smile stayed on his face.

"I never was lucky," he said. "Anyway, happy birthday, Lisa."

Then he kissed her, lightly, fleetingly on the lips. Like the brush of a butterfly wings, she tasted the warmth and sweetness of his mouth.

He moved away, calling to Grandpa about something, leaving her in the shadow of the tree, the moon glancing over her shoulder, putting a spell on everything, even the beat of her heart.

Chapter 13 _____

With only about ten days left on the farm, Lisa found herself going to the creek more and more. She anticipated this time alone. Before coming here, she had felt she wasn't living if she wasn't in the thick of things, surrounded with friends. Sometimes Jonas joined her, and they held serious discussions about bugs, the sky, jet airplanes, and how to get to her home in Centerville from his place.

It was a couple of days later when Charlie came by one afternoon.

"How about a movie tonight?" he asked.

She didn't really want to go, but he seemed so eager. "Okay."

He grinned happily. "Hey! That's great, Lisa. I'll be here about seven-thirty."

Grandma was pleased that she was going out with Charlie. "He's asked so many times. And he's such a nice boy, Lisa."

She kept her voice guarded. "He's okay, Grandma, but you know that Brad and I —"

"Oh, yes, Brad," she said.

"You did like him, didn't you?" Lisa asked anxiously.

"He has nice manners, and he's handsome. I can see why you might be interested in him."

But Grandma had evaded the question. It made her uneasy. First Mother and Dad and now Grandma. How could they all dislike Brad when she loved him so much?

She *did* love him! Sometimes, being here in the middle of nowhere, amid the tall rows of corn, she forgot that one basic fact. The festival hadn't been one of their better times together, but once home everything would fall into place. She had no doubt about that.

Charlie came on time, his old car purring down the lane and coming to a stop quietly. She had grown used to Kevin's wild driving and the skid of tires in the gravel.

"Hi, Tom!" Charlie called to Grandpa, the pup tagging at his heels.

"I'm getting attached to this pup," Grandpa told Charlie. "Even if Lisa decides to take him to Centerville, I think I'll try to talk her out of it. He sure is a lively one."

Charlie held the car door for her and helped her inside. In a moment, with a toot of the horn and a wave of his hand, they were off. He scarcely spoke all the way down the lane to the main road.

"You look really pretty tonight, Lisa," he said at last. "That's a peach of a dress."

She nodded her thanks, but couldn't find her voice. Was it going to be like this all evening? Heaven forbid. She began to fidget in the seat, and Charlie turned on the radio to some music. She tried to relax. The movie would be fun. Charlie would be fun. The entire evening would be one to remember if she could just forget about those blasted melons!

How could she? *But she must!*

The drive-in movie started at dusk. Charlie pulled The Heap into place and hung the speaker on the steering wheel where both of them could hear.

"Popcorn?" he asked. "And a Pepsi?"

"Sounds good."

"Be right back."

All through the movie and the previews of coming attractions, Lisa tried to be natural, to laugh when she was supposed to and to respond to anything Charlie said. He was being far too quiet. Not his usual self. This worried her.

When the movie was over, they joined the stream of cars out to the highway, and he drove away toward the city park. It was a large, shadowy place with fountains and flower beds. It overlooked the river, and Charlie wanted to get out of The Heap and sit on one of the benches.

"Or we can take a walk along one of the nature trails."

"In the dark?"

"There's a moon, and I know all the trails like the back of my hand. When I was a little kid, I loved to wander around here."

They left the car, and Charlie caught her hand in his. "We'll cross the foot bridge and sit over there, okay?"

The bridge spanned a trickle of water that came down from the bluffs overhead. Here, in a long forgotten yesterday, Indians had roamed and hunted and built council fires.

"I would like to have lived then," Charlie said.

"When?"

"When the Indians were here."

"That's funny. I was just thinking about that."

Charlie touched his forehead to hers. "Great minds run in the same channels."

His touch seemed to burn her. She pulled away. "Why would you want to be an Indian?" she asked.

"He was free."

"Aren't you?" she asked.

He laughed in the darkness. "Not like the Indian. He chased the wind if he wanted. But if I couldn't be an Indian, you know what my second choice would be?"

"I'd never guess."

"A sailor, with the sea for my home. Next to that I'd like to be a wildcatter looking for oil."

She shook her head. "I had no idea you had such wild dreams."

He shrugged. "Everyone has dreams. As long as you know that's all they are, a man can live with them. You're part of my dream too, Lisa."

She turned slightly away from him, hearing the serious note in his voice. A trembling started up inside.

"Lisa, I don't know just how to say this. So I'll say it right out. I'm in love with you. I want you to be my girl."

For a stunned moment she couldn't find her voice. She turned to him with an incredulous look on her face. "What did you say?"

He laughed awkwardly. "You heard me, Lisa. I wish I had the words to say it better. But I never was much good at that. So I told you like it is. I love you. I want you to be my girl."

He was bending his head toward her. She couldn't seem to move. There in the dark, in the shadows of the bluffs, with a summer breeze stirring giant oaks that were probably there even in the Indian days, Charlie kissed her.

He had never kissed her just like this before. It began gently, then grew with tenderness and fierceness until finally she broke away.

"You're special, Lisa. You know that?" he whispered.

"Charlie, don't do this. Please."

"Hush," he murmured. "Just hush. Let it happen."

He put his arm around her and pulled her along. They walked under the huge trees, following the worn path. Far away they heard the clack of a train's wheels over the tracks, saw a light on the river as a boat moved upstream. Damp pungent leaves, the river, the clean, sun-dried smell of Charlie's shirt — all of that was embedded in her memory like a diamond in the crust of the earth, waiting to be discovered.

Beside the cannon that overlooked the river — a sentinel in the night — they sat on the sun-warmed foundation, and Charlie pointed across the river.

"Straight across from here there was an Indian war once. They say the spring started flowing after the chief was killed, from the tears of his woman mourning for him."

"That's beautiful."

"Would you cry for me, Lisa?"

"Yes," she sighed. "I'd cry for you, Charlie."

"Then it's not zero?" he said with a note of hope in his voice.

"Charlie, I'll be going home soon."

"In eight days. I know."

"I won't be seeing you again."

"Centerville's not the end of the earth. I'll come and find you there."

"You don't understand," she said, despair welling up in her throat. "Charlie, don't make me hurt you!"

"You could never hurt me," he laughed. "I love you too much. I've loved you since that first day, Lisa. Even if you thought I must be something out of another world. I'll never forget the way you stared at me."

She flushed in embarrassment. "You were different, Charlie."

"Yeah," he confessed. "I still am. Does that bother you?"

"No. It makes you unique, Charlie Shaw."

He straightened. "But you don't love me."

She swallowed hard. "I think you'd better take me home. It's getting late, and you know Grandma."

He was very still for a moment. Then with a sigh he took her hand. "Okay. I'll take you now. I've had my say. Go home and sleep on it. Think about it."

Crazy Charlie! As if sleeping on it would change anything! And the one thing he had succeeded in doing was to rob her of any hope of sleep. It was impossible to close her eyes and drift off. The soft summer night seemed to sing to her with sighing branches and night sounds. Patterns of shadows on her wall flickered in quiet motion. Teddy barked briefly at a car on the far road and then went back to sleep. The puppy whined. Somewhere she thought she heard a jet airplane, and peering out the window, found its white trail streaking across the sky, illuminated by the moonlight. Unbearable loneliness swept over her and an ache she couldn't describe. If only she had never come here! How simple everything would have been.

Charlie came again the next evening. With Teddy and the puppy following them, they walked down to the stream. Charlie tried to teach her how to skip rocks across the water, but she didn't have the knack.

"Doesn't matter, you can still be my girl," he said with a grin.

He was giving her a significant look, waiting.

"I can't be your girl, Charlie," she said firmly.

He looked at her for a long time, letting her words sink in. "Because of Brad?"

"Partly," she admitted.

"What else?"

She thought she would never be able to get the words past her lips. "About your melon patch, Charlie. And the melons that were smashed the night before the festival . . ."

Charlie stiffened slightly; otherwise, he didn't move. But she knew he was listening intently. She rushed on, eager now to have her confession over and done.

"The Terrible Three did it," she said. "Brad and I helped."

He had turned to stone. She waited for him to lash out at her, to say some terrible thing to her, but he didn't say a word. The tears had started down her cheeks.

"I don't know why I let them. I didn't want them to do it, I wanted no part of it myself. But I just fell in with them, following Brad's lead, who was following Kevin's. Like dumb sheep, we just followed the leader. I hated it. I hated every minute of it!"

"Lisa —"

"But that doesn't change anything, does it?" she rushed on feverishly. "I did it, and I don't expect you to forgive me or to forget it. So, no, I can't be your girl, Charlie. I can't even be your friend!"

With that she turned and ran, stumbling through the growing darkness. Teddy came behind her, bringing the puppy. Once she thought she heard Charlie call to her, but she wasn't certain. She didn't stop to see. She just ran, gulping in deep breaths, wishing she felt purified by her confession, but she didn't. Nothing would ever erase her shame and guilt.

Chapter 14 _____

Lisa's last day on the farm was perfect. She awakened refreshed. Looking out the window, she saw the rolling fields and knew that within another six weeks or so the harvest would be starting. Her heart ached to think that Grandpa's yield would be so short because of the windstorm. But already he was looking ahead to the next year.

She helped Grandma with the flower beds and the garden. After lunch, she and the dogs went down to the stream, where she found Jonas waiting for her. With a laugh she swept him up in her arms and put a kiss on his warm cheek.

It was a bittersweet time. Each moment was precious. She laughed and romped with Jonas, and when he grew sleepy, she let him curl up with his head in her lap. She fingered his dark curls and studied the long silky length of his lashes. Such a dear little boy. Someday she'd like a child like him. Someday — that was far in the future yet. There was high school to finish, college, a career. Dad wanted her to study medicine, but she felt she had no inclination for that. Jody couldn't understand her reasons for wanting to stay away from the hospital.

What was her destiny? She didn't really know. Sometimes she thought she'd like to be a writer or a designer of some kind. High fashion model — or a radio announcer. A dozen possibilities had drifted in and out of her head at various times. Surely soon there would be a sign, something would trigger off a response inside her so that she would find her way. Now she was floating at loose ends. She was just Lisa — Brad's Lisa — content to be the other half of the golden couple at Centerville High School. Brad. She would see him tomorrow. He would probably meet her bus. The summer was over, and they would pick up where they left off.

The thought made her uneasy, and she didn't know why, didn't try to analyze it. Not now. Not on this last perfect day in the country.

Jonas awakened after a while and said he had to go home. He gave her a wet kiss and another hug.

"I'll see you again before I go," she promised.

For another half hour she enjoyed the solitude of the stream. She wanted to remember everything about it — the twisted oak, the weeping willow with its branches nearly touching the water, the path down to the stream, the patch where wild violets bloomed, the sweet smell of wild roses on a nearby fence, and more than anything, the sky. The wide, deep, immense sky that stretched from her heart to infinity. What was beyond what the eye could see? What deep dark holes were there in space and what was out there?

She went back to the house, and Grandma had fixed a very special supper with all Lisa's favorites.

148

They tried to be happy and carefree, but all of them realized it was her last supper here.

When the phone rang, she knew it was going to be Charlie.

"I won't take no for an answer," he said. "I have to see you again. Let's have this one last date. Okay?"

Her head told her no, but her heart said yes. "All right, Charlie."

"I'll come by about eight."

Lisa rushed to help clear the table and do the dishes. After changing her clothes, she went out to wait for Charlie on the back step. The Heap soon rattled into view, and Charlie got out with a grin on his face.

"If you're ready, let's get the show on the road."

"Where are we going?"

"I don't know. I'm open for suggestions."

They got into the old car, and Charlie started the motor. They waved to her grandparents and drove away down the lane. At the main road Charlie looked at her with a smile.

"Right or left?"

"Left. Let's not go to Reynolds or Bloomhurst. Let's go somewhere new."

"Gotcha," Charlie nodded.

She was glad when Charlie drove toward the lake and parked the car near the water.

"Want to walk?"

"Yes."

They found an empty bench overlooking the lake, and they sat there, not touching.

"Charlie, I have to say something. About your melons . . . I'm going to pay back every penny. I'll save my allowance and get a job after school. You'll get back every cent, Charlie."

"You weren't the only one that smashed my melons," he pointed out.

"It doesn't matter. It's the only way I can live with myself. It's the only way we can ever be friends, Charlie Shaw."

He put his hands around her face and smiled at her through the growing darkness. "Friends?" he asked. "It's more with me. I told you that, Lisa. I love you."

He lowered his head, and his mouth found hers in a sweet, tender kiss.

"How can you love me?" she whispered. "After what I did to you?"

"Love has blinders, don't you know that? This old hard-headed mule can only see one thing, and that's you, Lisa, and the fact that I love you."

"Charlie, you're so special!" she said with a touch of awe in her voice. "I never realized until this very moment just how really special you are."

"Does that mean you love me?" he asked quietly, hopefully.

She touched his face with her fingertips. "I'm not sure. Perhaps I do. I need time, Charlie."

He nodded. "You've got all the time you need, Lisa. I can wait. I'd wait a lifetime for you."

She began to cry, and Charlie kissed away her tears. "Don't cry, Lisa. Don't cry."

"But it's all so sad and beautiful at the same time. How can that be?"

"I don't know."

"I want to go home, and yet I want to stay. I

want to be with you, and yet I'm afraid to be, Charlie."

"I know. I feel the same way. Sometimes it scares me to death the way I feel about you. I'm afraid to touch you sometimes, afraid you'll vanish into thin air and just be a beautiful dream. Other times I *need* to touch you, to have you in my arms, to hear you laugh and see your eyes flash. What do you think it is, Lisa?"

"Some would say it's growing up."

"I'd say it was love," he replied.

"Love," she murmured.

"Sweet love."

"Tomorrow I'll be miles away."

"Tomorrow I'll die a little," he answered.

"Will you come to Centerville?"

"Try and keep me away. I'll come Christmas."

"Christmas!"

"I'll miss you, Lisa, but I'll love you more every minute."

"Christmas," she sighed. "It's so long to wait."

Chapter 15 _____

Everyone was there to see her off the next morning. Grandma was hiding her tears, and Grandpa was talking about something no one was interested in. Lennie shook her hand, and Sue hugged her. Jonas clung to her until the last minute. Charlie didn't kiss her or touch her, but his love was in his eyes.

"Christmas," he promised. "I'll see you then."

The bus driver was waiting. With a last-minute flurry of hugs and kisses and shouts of goodbye, Lisa boarded. In a moment the bus lurched away. From the window she saw the small group of people huddled together, waving to her. Her heart ached at the sight of them, and then with determination she thought ahead to the end of her journey. Home. It would be good to be home again. The summer was over. Time to get on with her life once more.

Brad wasn't there to meet her. But her mother came rushing to her. "Lisa! It's so good to see you!"

"Where's Brad?"

"I haven't seen him," Mother answered with a quick frown. "How are you, dear?"

"I'm fine," Lisa said vaguely, annoyed that Brad had not made the effort to meet her bus. Surely he wasn't *that* busy.

On the way home, Lisa listened as her mother told her all about Paris and what she had done here.

"Your father has promised to be home early. We'll have dinner together so we can catch up on everything."

Lisa unpacked her things, marveling at the size of her room and the luxury of it. She'd forgotten it was so nice.

Her father looked tired when he came, but he seemed genuinely glad to see her. He hugged her hard and pushed her back for a long look. "You've blossomed. How lovely you are!"

Of course, their dinner was interrupted by an emergency at the hospital, and her father rushed away with the usual apology.

"Back in the old groove," Lisa sighed.

"Too bad," Mother replied sympathetically.

The next phone call was for Mother, an old friend anxious to hear about her trip. Lisa was forgotten. With a sigh she realized that this would never have happened at Grandma's house. They always had time for her. They had grown close. Wistfully she wished this were true with her parents.

Once they *had* been close. Then, as Lisa had grown older, she'd become fiercely independent and defensive. She realized now it had been all her doing. It was something she had *made* happen!

With a frown, disliking the thought, she went to her room to use her telephone. Dialing Brad's number, she waited anxiously for the sound of his voice. But no one answered. Where was he?

Of course! Football practice.

Calling to her mother that she was going out, Lisa hurried to the school. The football field was ablaze with lights, and she could see the team on the turf. With a lift of her heart she spotted Brad, his wide shoulders immense under the harness and uniform of the Centerville team. Several kids gathered to watch.

"Lisa!"

It was Jody. Lisa frowned. Wouldn't you know the first person she would see would be Jody!

Jody gave her a shy grin. "I'm glad you're back. It seemed funny knowing that you weren't over there at your house."

"I suppose you've been busy."

"At the hospital," Jody nodded. "It's been a good summer. What about you?"

"Better than I'd hoped," she admitted.

She was holding her breath, waiting for Jody to start up about the wonderful attributes of working at the hospital, and she didn't have to wait long.

"I really wish you'd consider it," Jody finished, giving her that warmhearted smile of hers.

Lisa shook her head. "I'm sorry, Jody. I think it's great what you're doing. I really do. I wish I had the knack. But I don't, and I know it."

Jody looked at her with a touch of surprise. "You don't seem quite so defensive about it now."

Lisa shrugged. "No. I guess I've changed, Jody."

Jody grinned. "We all do."

Another look at Jody and Lisa realized that she had matured over the summer. She was still shy, but there was a new strength about her. Charlie flashed through her mind. They *were* the same kind of people!

"Listen, want to join my friends and me?" Jody asked. "We're over there on the far side of the bleachers."

"Not tonight, Jody," Lisa said, more kindly than she had in the past. "I want to see Brad the minute he comes off the field. Another time."

Jody squeezed her hand. "Sure."

Jody moved away, and Lisa turned her attention to the players. She heard shouts of encouragement from the sidelines, and one girl in particular seemed to be calling to Brad constantly. When the practice ended a few minutes later, Lisa was waiting at the end of the field for him. He saw her at once and came jogging toward her. He gave her an awkward hug and smiled down at her.

"I couldn't meet your bus, sorry. I had to report to practice at four, and you know the coach — he eats quarterbacks for breakfast!"

She laughed, for suddenly everything was all right. "Oh, Brad, it's good to be home again!"

"Better believe it. Listen, I'll shower and be out in a flash. How about the Pizza Palace? The team's going there. Okay?"

"Yes."

She wondered where Randy and Tammy were and didn't have to wait long. They pulled up in Randy's car and shouted to her.

"Hey, Lisa!" Tammy called.

"Man, you're a sight for sore eyes," Randy grinned.

They were so busy catching up on the things that had happened all summer long that Brad was there before Lisa expected him. He put his arm around her and motioned for Randy to drive on.

"Let's move it out, fella."

"Yeah, yeah, your audience awaits you, your highness," Randy said wryly.

Everyone laughed. Nothing had changed.

Lisa had forgotten the adulation that Brad always brought wherever he went. Over pizzas they were quickly and easily the center of attention while Brad explained about a long pass he had thrown during an important game last season.

The talk went on and on about Brad's wonderful prowess on the field. Lisa stirred restlessly, bored with the conversation, and surprised that she was. Before she had always hung on to every word Brad spoke. Now suddenly she realized he was far more self-centered than she'd noticed before. Brad was smooth about it all, but had a way of always turning the conversation back to himself. He did it so cleverly that even Randy and Tammy didn't realize what was happening.

It was late when they finally took Lisa home. Brad saw Lisa to the door and kissed her for a long moment.

"See you tomorrow, beautiful."

"Yes."

Then he was gone. Inside the light burned, and Mother was still up. She looked angry.

"Have you looked at the time, Lisa?"

"No. Sorry. Is it *that* late?"

"Yes, it is. Your father came home early from the hospital, planning to spend the evening with you."

She couldn't blame them for being angry. "I'm sorry. It won't happen again, Mother."

Her mother was caught off guard by the sincerity in Lisa's voice.

Lisa did not sleep well that night. It seemed so strange here. So noisy. The traffic went by the house all night long. Lisa twisted and turned. She thumped her pillow. She thought about Brad. Tomorrow — he'd see her tomorrow.

Yes, of course. Everything was the same. Absolutely the same. So why wasn't she happier? There was no need for guilt. Charlie had no strings on her. He knew she would see Brad. She *had* been dying to see him again. Well, now the big moment was past. It hadn't been what she expected and she didn't know what she had hoped for.

School started, and in the hectic next few days it seemed nothing had changed at all. There was only one fly in the ointment. Everywhere she turned, it seemed Shelia Whitman was hanging around. She found excuses to talk to Brad, and one night after practice she joined them in the big booth at one of their favorite hangouts. Shelia had eyes only for Brad, and Brad laughed with her and gave her a look that sent Lisa's heart churning. They did not speak of her for several days, and then suddenly, over nothing, a quarrel erupted.

"You're not the Lisa I used to know," Brad said angrily. "What's with you these days?"

"What's with you and Shelia Whitman?" she fired back.

Brad blinked and set his jaw. "She's a friend. A great kid. That's not what we're talking about, Lisa. We're talking about this attitude of yours."

"What attitude?"

"Well, I hate to say it, Lisa, but you're getting more square every day. I'd almost think you were hanging out with Jody again."

Fury burned through her, hot and out of control. "Don't criticize Jody. She's a decent, unselfish girl!"

Brad shook his head with despair. "She's a drag, and you know it, Lisa. I thought we saw alike on that."

"You know what I think?" she asked hotly. "I think you only care about yourself and your own self-importance."

A cold, steely look came to Brad's face. For a long, uncomfortable moment they stared at each other. She swallowed hard, stunned that she had said such a terrible thing.

"If that's the case, then perhaps it's time I found someone who appreciates me and who doesn't say such horrible lies about me!"

With that Brad turned on his heel and stalked away. Lisa felt alternately sick and relieved. Days passed. A week. Two weeks. Now Shelia was often seen in Brad's company, hanging to his arm, glowing like a neon light whenever she looked at him. With a fleeting thought Lisa realized that she had acted the very same way.

It was soon all over school that they were Splitsville, and Jody came over one evening to talk to her about it. "You must feel awful."

"No," Lisa said, taking a deep breath. "I don't. Oh, I'll miss him. There were things about Brad that were special — in some ways he'll always be special to me — but I've got to look ahead, make plans.

"What kinds of plans?" Jody asked.

Lisa shook her head. "I'm not sure yet. But I'll get a job, do something I really like. I've got some ideas, but I want to talk them over with my folks first."

"Not the hospital?"

Lisa laughed. "No. Give up, Jody. I know I don't belong there. But there's a job at the newspaper office. Nothing glamorous. A kind of errand girl. I think it would really be exciting to work around a newspaper. I'd like to apply for that."

"Sounds fun," Jody agreed. "Hey, if you get the job, we'll celebrate. I've got the weekend off. We could go shopping or something. Have lunch at Cheever's Department Store, like we used to."

"Okay!" Lisa nodded. "It's a date."

She went to find her mother as soon as Jody had gone.

"Mother —"

She was in the kitchen, checking a roast in the oven. "Your father's due in half an hour," Mother said.

"Unless there's an emergency," Lisa sighed.

"It's the way it is with a doctor. He doesn't like it any better than we do."

"Well, if he's late, let's wait for him."

Mother wiped her hands on a towel and looked at her for a pensive moment. "You mean you have no plans to go out tonight?"

"You might as well know, it's over with Brad."

Mother tried hard not to show her relief, but it was there in the sudden sag of her shoulders. "What happened? Want to talk about it?"

"He's just not for me. He's . . . different . . . no, it's *me* that's different."

"I'm sorry, baby. I know it's hard sometimes when these things happen."

Lisa gave her mother a quick hug. "I'll survive. I've got something to talk over with you and Dad. Maybe after dinner?" Lisa asked.

"Of course! Is it important?"

"Very," she nodded.

Dinner was late because her father was late. But it didn't matter. He was happy to find her there and gave her a surprised look. But Dad was tactful, and he didn't ask questions. Mother would tell him the news about Brad later. At the right moment Lisa told them about the job.

"It's at the newspaper office. I want to apply. I just hope it's still there. It won't pay much, I know. I heard the hours would be from four until six. I could handle that after school. The thing is, it's something I want to do. I just hope that you'll understand."

Dad looked disappointed, and she knew he was thinking about Jody's work at the hospital.

"Dad, I can't be what you want. I'm sorry. I'm just not cut out for it. I want to find my own place. I need the chance to look."

Dad reached out and patted her hand with a grin. "You're absolutely right. Give the job a try. You may or may not like it," he cautioned. "But you should find out."

With a whoop of delight Lisa rushed around the table to give him a hug and to kiss her mother. "Hey, you know, you're the greatest!"

Dad leaned back with a touch of sadness on his face. "By golly, I believe my little girl is growing up."

The next day Lisa went to apply for the job, relieved to find that it hadn't been filled. The pay was even worse than she had imagined, and this had probably kept some of the other kids away. But she was ready to try, and the editor, a big, graying man with glasses, eyed her up and down for a long moment.

"You're Dr. Holden's daughter?"

"Yes."

"I'll work you hard."

"I'll handle it," she said confidently. "Please, give me a chance to try."

The editor grinned. "Spunky, I see. Well, always admired spunk when it's handled right. Okay, you're on. Report to work tomorrow after school."

She couldn't wait to tell Jody! She rushed straight home to tell Mother and then went next door to find Jody.

Jody was waiting for her and opened the door with a look of hope on her face.

"I got the job!" Lisa said before she could ask.

They danced a jig together and made plans for their celebration.

Lisa eagerly awaited her first paycheck, and when she got it, she sent all but a few dollars to Charlie. There! The first payment had been made against the ruined melons. She began to feel better already.

The homecoming football game was a big event at Centerville. They had a tough opponent in Springdale. When Brad came racing onto the field with the team, Lisa felt a strange wave of nostalgia. It seemed odd not to be sitting in the front row. He had always wanted her where he could see her, but she noticed that Shelia Whitman was there now.

"Any regrets?" Jody asked.

She shook her head. "No."

"I know a couple of other boys asked you to go with them," Jody said.

"Wasn't interested. I think I care about someone I met during the summer. I'm not ready for anyone else just yet. Charlie is still on my mind."

"Do you think it's him all the way?" Jody asked.

"Who knows? When I see him again, maybe I'll find that he's not nearly as attractive as I thought. Maybe it was summer madness — who knows? Time has a way of changing everything."

Centerville won the game, thanks to Brad's wonderful athletic powers. The fans went wild. At the Pizza Palace with Jody, Lisa saw that the huge table in the corner had been saved for Brad as usual. When he came in with Randy and Tammy, Shelia was on his arm. As Lisa watched, she saw how the others went rushing up to Brad to shake his hand or thump him on the back. Invitations were flying for him to visit this table or that or to attend someone's party.

Brad, noble and handsome, shook his head and turned his attention to his favored friends. The king was reigning. Lisa turned away. Brad seemed so shallow, so stuck on himself. She knew he was good at football and baseball and nearly every other sport he tried. Brad was the golden boy, and now Shelia was the golden girl.

Somehow, to Lisa, their glitter seemed tarnished.

Chapter 16 —————————

With the end of the football season autumn was over, and the cold winds of December had begun to blow through Centerville, reminding Lisa that Christmas was growing closer and closer.

She and Jody went Christmas-shopping together, laughing and having a great time. Funny, why had she ever thought Jody shy and backward? She was quiet, but her sense of humor was keener than most. They confided in one another and spent most of their spare time together.

Grandma wrote that they would be driving to Centerville for the Christmas holiday and that they would bring Charlie with them.

"Mother, you're going to find him . . . different," Lisa warned.

"From what I hear of him, he's a very nice boy. I'm anxious to meet him."

But what would Charlie really think of her parents, and her home, which was elaborate by anyone's standards? Would it put him off? Oh, but it shouldn't. Friends were friends, no matter what their background. And Dad was easy to talk to. Somehow he would put Charlie at ease, if need be.

She was, frankly, on pins and needles. Even the hectic work at the newspaper didn't keep her from thinking about it. Summer seemed so long ago now. So much had happened since then. What if the magic was gone? What if she found him *too* different? Well, time would tell.

Jody told her to stop worrying. "Everything works out eventually, one way or another."

At least she had managed to pay back most of the money for the melons. The last payment would be tucked into Charlie's Christmas gift. Dad had helped her pick out the set of tools in a hardware store.

"Any man would like those," he said. "I used to tinker with autos a little myself. I wish I had time for it now. I've got a rattle in my car — maybe Charlie can help me locate the trouble over the holidays."

Lisa could have hugged him. He was going to make Charlie feel at home.

The newspaper office closed early the day before Christmas. There had been no school, so she had helped Mother decorate the house and bake another batch of cookies. Everything looked festive, and when two o'clock came, Lisa found herself watching the clock. They should be coming any minute now. What would she say to him? How would he look? What if, at the last minute, he decided not to come.

There, was that the sound of a car door slamming? She went to peer out the window. "They're here! Mother, they're here!"

Grandpa was helping Grandma out of the car, and Charlie was half hidden, bringing packages out of the trunk, loading his arms with them.

Lisa ran to open the door. In the excitement of greeting, with hugs and kisses and everyone talking at once, it was a moment or two before she found herself looking up into Charlie's good-natured grin. Could it be he was taller than ever? And just as thin? But he seemed older somehow, less boyish. His eyes were clear and bright, studying her intently. He wore no hat, so his thick hair was mussed by the wind. With his coat collar turned up, his nose red with the cold, he brought the scent of fresh air with him.

"Hi, Lisa," he said.

She'd forgotten the soft timbres of his voice and the depth of it. With an embarrassed laugh she plucked the boxes from his arms. "Put them under the tree, Charlie, before you drop everything."

Mother welcomed him warmly and told him to make himself at home. He was wearing new shoes, shined like mirrors. A blue tie was knotted loosely, and the sleeves of his coat were a little short. Oh, but he was Charlie, just as she remembered him.

"You look great, Lisa," he said. "I knew you were pretty, but you seem prettier than ever."

"There you go already!" she teased.

He caught her hand in his, and for a warm moment a tingle raced between them.

"It's been a long time," he said. "I was afraid when Christmas came, you wouldn't want me to come."

"And I was afraid you'd decide not to come."

"No such luck. You're stuck with me, Lisa!"

"How is everyone? How is Jonas?"

"He wanted to come with me."

"Oh — why didn't you bring him?"

"I'm a selfish sort of guy," Charlie answered. "I didn't want to share you with anyone. He loves you, you know. And he carries your letters around until they about fall to pieces."

"The family must hate having you away for Christmas."

"It's okay, Lisa. We celebrated before I left. What's another day or so anyway?"

Christmas Eve dinner at the Holden house had always been oyster stew, stalks of celery, and a rich dessert. It was no different this time, and when Dad came home he was beaming happily.

"Glad you could come, all of you. Next year I'm going to come to the farm, Tom. No matter what. Time I spent some holidays with my family where I want to spend them."

"Famous last words," Grandpa laughed.

"No. I'll arrange it," Dad said firmly. "Would you like that, Lisa? Christmas on the farm?"

"I'd love it!"

Charlie and Lisa's father hit it off at once. When they came to the table a few minutes later, they were discussing the proper motor oil to use and the importance of regular tune-ups. Grandpa gave Lisa a grin and Grandma squeezed her hand. With a happy sigh Lisa bowed her head while Dad gave the prayer.

It was decided they couldn't wait until morning to open presents.

"Christmas Eve is just as good," Dad said.

"Look, it's snowing!" Charlie said.

"Right on cue," Grandpa laughed.

"Let's take a walk, Charlie," Lisa said. "As soon as we open our presents."

"You're on!"

The presents were passed out by Grandpa, who had always done it and would be hurt if he wasn't allowed to do it this year. Lisa watched slyly as Charlie opened his gift and smiled when she saw the pleased and happy look on his face.

"Lisa, these tools are great! Boy, do I need them!"

"I'm glad you like them."

Charlie's gift to her was in a tiny box. When she opened it, she found a charming little locket on a fine golden chain.

"Delicate and beautiful like you," he told her. "I hope you like it."

"I love it!"

There were practical gifts from her grandparents, more Paris clothes from her parents. When the excitement had died down at last and the debris of wrapping paper and ribbon was picked up, Lisa went to get her coat.

"Let's go for a walk now, Charlie."

"Bundle up," Grandpa instructed. "It's cold out there.

They stamped into snow boots, snuggled into warm coats and scarves, and went out into the crisp, snowy night. The flakes were huge and settled on Charlie's black hair.

"Where's your hat?"

"Don't wear one," he said.

"You should, you'll catch a cold."

"Okay, okay," he laughed. "I've got a cap in here somewhere."

From one of the large overcoat pockets he brought out a fur, Russian-style, hat and put it on his head.

"You look dashing."

"Clothes make the man," he sighed. "Sue gave it to me for Christmas. I thought I looked a little silly in it."

"You do not!" she insisted. "Sue has excellent taste."

"You taught her a lot," Charlie said seriously. "She wants to be like you."

"Oh, dear —"

"I think it's great," Charlie said.

They passed under a street light, and she saw the glow in his eyes.

"You know, you never kissed me hello," Lisa said.

"I wasn't sure that I should."

He put his arms around her and pulled her close. His warm mouth was on hers, and for the strangest moment she was back at the farm — it was summertime, and the skies were blue with fleecy white clouds. Time had turned backward.

"Oh, Lisa, it's the same. It's the same!" he said with awe.

"Were you worried it wouldn't be?" she asked.

"A little."

They walked on, arm in arm, and the snow beneath their boots crunched and squeaked. They walked for blocks, talking, catching up, laughing at old memories.

When they got to the skating rink at the park, they thought of trying their luck.

"Not tonight," Charlie decided. "Maybe tomorrow."

At one of the benches he brushed the snow aside, and they sat there huddling together. They watched the skaters, and Charlie left long enough to buy them two steaming cups of hot chocolate at the refreshment stand.

"I like your folks," he said.

"I'm glad. I like them, too. We're closer now. For a while there, we drifted apart."

"You like your job, don't you?"

"I could rave on and on about it, I love it," she laughed.

"As long as you're happy. That's what counts, Lisa."

"Do you think some day I'll be a well-known reporter for some big newspaper?"

"Oh, a TV celebrity probably," he teased.

"And you?"

He took a moment to answer. "Who knows? I've told you how it is with me. I think I'd like to own a garage someday. But I don't have stars in my eyes, Lisa. You do."

"Charlie —"

"Do you think it will work with us? We've got a lot of odds against us."

"Don't talk like that!"

"We're very different. Sometimes that's a drawback."

She knew he was right. It might come to nothing. But now, for this heartbeat, it was everything, and "now" was what counted.

"Why are we being so serious on Christmas Eve?" she asked lightly.

He laughed. "Who knows? Hey, I'll race you over to that street light. Loser has to pay off with a kiss."

They sped away with a laugh, and Charlie's longer legs easily outdistanced hers. She was winded when she caught up with him. He wouldn't leave until she kissed him.

Then he dropped his arm around her shoulder, and they wandered on, listening to the Christmas bells chiming into the cold night. They stopped at a little cafe she and Jody often visited. It was still open, and there, despite the dinner they'd eaten at home, they devoured sandwiches and Pepsis.

The owner was anxious to close. Charlie seemed in no hurry. From his pocket he took out a small envelope and pressed it into her hand.

"Another Christmas present," he said.

"What on earth is it?"

"Open it and see," he laughed.

She tore open the envelope. Pouring the contents out, she saw the watermelon seeds, black oval specks, lying dormant in the palm of her hand.

He closed her fingers over them.

"Come plant them with me next summer," he said.

"Charlie! Only you would give a girl watermelon seeds!"

His eyes were tender and gentle. "It's our promise of summer, Lisa. We'll plant the seeds together. Watch them grow — okay?"

She clutched the seeds tightly. A promise of summer. What a wonderful thought, what an idea to cling to through the winter and the long spring until school was out and she was free again.

"Charlie Shaw, I love you."

"And I love you, Lisa. Summer," he whispered. "Until summertime."

Returning the seeds to the envelope, Lisa tucked them securely into her pocket. They left the cafe and went back into the night, turning toward home.

Her shoulder fit snugly under his arm. Their steps went along in unison. Crisp stars twinkled at them. The same stars shown down on Reynolds and Grandpa and Grandma's house. They twinkled in the woods and on the stream, frozen now and sleeping, along with the wild violets and yellow buttercups. It all waited for her. She felt the seeds in her pocket and smiled. A promise of summer.